THE PERFECT CATCH

BRITNEY M. MILLS

CRYSTAL CANYON PUBLISHING

CHAPTER 1

KATE

I made it through the line in the cafeteria, grabbing the breadsticks the local pizza place sold during lunch. From the look of the main menu, I was just glad I had enough money in my wallet to cover it. My mom always put money into the lunch accounts for my freshman brother, Zane, and me, but there were some days when not even the pizza looked edible. Today was one of those days.

To be honest, I was surprised she'd finally stopped making paper bag lunches for us. Zane and I had both begged several times to just let us get something at school, but it wasn't until the start of this year that she actually did. It saved me the money I used to buy my own anyway.

Finding my group of friends over at our usual table in the middle of the lunchroom, I weaved in and out of chairs that hadn't been pushed in, the backpack I'd slung over one shoulder bumping along them as I passed.

When I arrived at the table, I dropped the backpack on the ground and slumped into the seat, grateful for the moment to breathe.

Penny glanced up from her chef salad and grimaced. "Calc that bad again?"

I nodded. "I don't think I'll ever remember what Mr. Giles taught us for the last ninety minutes, and I'm pretty sure it'll be fifty percent of the next test."

"Hey, Kate," someone called over my shoulder.

I turned, a ready smile on my face as I waved. It took a second for me to register that it was one of the sophomores I'd worked with in a group during choir. Laura? Linda? One of the downsides to being the student body president was that I had to either know or fake that I knew people's names.

"How are you?" I called, hoping her name and some of the other details about her would come to me. I'd been an officer at Rosemont High for the past three years, and while I'd gotten to know a lot of the students, sometimes I thought my brain was at max capacity. Maybe it was the fallout from having math right before lunch.

The girl was almost down the hall and yelled, "Good!" She waved and turned the corner.

"That was the most original conversation I've ever heard," Serena said, sliding her tray onto the table and sitting next to me.

Brynn moved to the other side of the table, giggling. "That's what happens when you become student body president. People are excited to talk to you and then don't have much else to say."

I balled up the wrapper from my straw and threw it at her. "Come on, it's not that bad. I get to plan cool dances and events for you guys. And here you are, not appreciating it." I laughed, and the other girls joined in.

We were such an eclectic group. Penny was a softball player, Serena played volleyball, and Brynn had been the starting center for the women's basketball team since she was a freshman. I'd been a dancer up until I got into high school, but I realized I liked teaching more than panicking when it came to competitions. Somehow, we made our different talents work. It gave us plenty of time to enjoy the other's activities.

"Speaking of dances," I said, smiling widely at my friends, "you're all planning on going to the next one, right?" I looked around at each of them, hoping they would nod and agree emphatically. I'd have even taken an unenthusiastic shoulder shrug at that point.

"It's the Harvest dance, Kate," Brynn said, twirling her spaghetti around her fork. "We just went to homecoming."

I tapped the table a couple of times and nodded. "Yes, but homecoming was guys-ask. Come on, girls. Please say at least two of you are going so I don't have to join the officer group." I clapped my fingers together and intertwined them, doing my best to plead with my mind and facial expression.

Penny laughed. "Let me guess, Stacy Waterhouse wants you to go to an escape room."

I pointed at her and said, "Yes, yes she does. We already did that for homecoming since I didn't get to go in the awesome baseball group with you two." I pointed at Penny, who'd gone with her boyfriend, Jake, and Serena, who'd gone with her newish boyfriend, Ben.

"I can't make it," Serena said, opening her carton of chocolate milk. "My mom and I have an event for the boutique that day." She'd started working with her mom to build their clothing boutique a few weeks before, and it sounded like the company was growing and fast. I'd even contemplated working for them, if I had a clear schedule. As it was, my planner, if I had one, would be black with ink.

"I already asked Jake." Penny waggled her eyebrows, and we chuckled.

"I was thinking about asking a guy in one of my classes.

Garrett Park?" Brynn looked around at all of us, and I nodded.

"He plays football, right?" I asked, giving her a cheesy grin. With Brynn's height, it was sometimes difficult for her to find a date who was either her height or taller, so the fact that she was thinking about asking someone was a plus.

She nodded. "He's pretty chill, and I think he'd be fun for whatever we decide to do for the day activity."

"Who are you taking, Kate?" Penny asked. They all leaned in like it would be some state secret. She smiled even wider, the mischief revealing itself. "No luck finding the guy in the mask yet?"

I leaned back in my chair, staring up at the ceiling for several seconds. When I sat back up, breaking off a piece of my breadstick, I shook my head. "No. I'm pretty sure he goes to another school. I would have found him by now, right?"

The Masked Kisser. The guy who'd gone to a party last spring wearing a mask a la Zorro and at one point leaned down and kissed me, on the lips. I tried to downplay it for my friends, but they could read me too easily. I'd only kissed one other guy in my life—Johnny Fisher, freshman year. It was a sweet little peck on the lips, but that was it—until the end of my junior year. I don't know if it was just that I didn't kiss a lot, but I was pretty sure I could still feel the electricity in my lips from the Masked Kisser every time I thought about it.

"You'd think it'd be easier to figure out who he is since your mother hears and sees everything at this school," Serena said, chewing on a fry. Truer words had never been spoken. My mother was the epitome of helicopter mom.

"I just wish we'd seen him kiss you. Maybe we'd be able to tell you who he was." Brynn had this weird talent where she could recognize people from the back of them, probably some perk to seeing above the crowd. If there was a way to teleport back to that moment just to move her into position, I would do it.

Opening my to-do list, I added *Ask someone to dance* to the list and clicked the phone back off. "I'll have to figure that out."

The table was silent for a few minutes before voices yelled over my shoulder. I turned around, glancing out to a large group of people standing around something in the commons.

I told myself it shouldn't matter who was in the middle of the mob, that I should just finish my lunch and move on with my day. My mom had given me several lectures on appearances and how things could look, no matter how innocent. And yet I still stood, walking with my three friends over to the outskirts of the group. I stretched up on my tiptoes, trying to see who was in the middle. Fists flew, and at least one of them connected with a jaw, jerking Trent Jacobs's head to the side with a weird cracking sound.

I could only see the back of the guy who'd thrown the punch, sandy-brown hair and broad shoulders. For a second, I wondered if he was my Masked Kisser because he was so tall and big. But then again, everyone was tall and big compared to my five feet and half an inch.

Seconds went by before the crowd on the other side parted as Principal McKee and Mrs. Watkins barged through, assessing the damage and pulling the two guys apart. Mr. McKee was lucky Trent didn't nail him with a punch as he tried to hit his opponent after the last one.

"Everyone get to fourth period," Mr. McKee said, his tone harsh, but it worked. Students dispersed throughout the commons and halls, the bell ringing a few seconds after his words.

I watched the two kids being led down the hall to the

principal's office and wondered what had spurred them to fight.

"Here's your backpack and your last breadstick," Penny said, stepping next to me again. I hadn't realized she'd gone to retrieve them, but then again, she hated being late to anything.

"Thanks," I said, waving goodbye as I walked up the stairs in the direction of my next class: Senior Committee. My mind wouldn't leave the scene I'd witnessed, and I kept seeing the back of the guy walking down the hall, no matter how much I tried to swipe it away. Being the president of the student body, I knew when new students moved into Rosemont High, so he definitely wasn't new. I was going to blame it on the little sleep I'd gotten over the past couple of days and not on the fact that I was more than curious.

CHAPTER 2

DAX

Sitting with my head in my hands, I listened to the monotone hum of the principal's voice through the door. I'd been waiting for over ten minutes, and if it weren't for the secretary with eyes in the back of her head, I'd have gotten up and walked out by now. My jaw still stung from the hit I'd taken from Trent Jacobs, and it would probably end up bruised. Not like I hadn't had to hide that kind of thing before.

I wasn't someone special at this school, and if it weren't for the chance to play baseball, I probably would have dropped out a while ago. But Mr. McKee and my grandmother, Noni, wouldn't let that happen.

The door opened, and Trent walked out, shooting me a smirk. A ring of bluish-black ran around one eye and down into his cheek. At least he didn't get out of the fight unscathed. The kid gave me a wide berth, and if I hadn't heard my name from the principal, I would have tried to continue what we'd started in the commons.

"Come in, Dax," the principal said, his voice sounding

wearier every time I was called in. Once I stepped inside, he motioned to a chair. "Sit."

Taking a deep breath, I slouched down into the uncomfortable wooden excuse for a chair in his office, the familiar smell of microwaved food wafting through the room. Garlic. Pasta. It made my stomach grumble just thinking about it. All I'd had for lunch was a mushy apple I'd grabbed on my way out the door that morning.

Principal McKee leaned forward, his glasses set halfway down his nose for the signature "I don't want to tell you again" look. I stretched out my legs, ready for the lecture I probably deserved.

"Dax, this is the second time in six weeks that you've sat in my office, not to mention last year and the year before that. I've always tried to give you the benefit of the doubt since you lost your mother, but this is getting old. I thought you were going to make an effort to change." He pulled his glasses off with one hand and rubbed his nose and the corner of his eyes with his thumb and forefinger.

A shot of guilt flowed through me, and I sat up, leaning my elbows on my thighs. Studying the back of my hands, I nodded. "I'm sorry, Mr. McKee. Trent was running his mouth, and I just…I couldn't hold back." I made a fist as if I could deal him one last blow, even though he'd left a few minutes ago. I paused for a minute, glancing up at Mr. McKee. He usually got straight to the point. "What's the punishment this time?"

Shaking his head, Mr. McKee said, "That's the problem, Dax. There shouldn't be a 'this time'." He pursed his lips, his eyes seeing right through me. Several seconds passed before he spoke again. "I tried calling your father but only got his voicemail."

I nodded. "He's on the road this week. He said something about being home tomorrow." As I said the words, dread pooled through me as it did just about every time my father came home from driving his truck.

"Since the previous punishments haven't changed much for you, I think we'll do something different this time." He flipped through a few papers on his desk, tapping his finger against his lips as he did so. "Senior Committee is always looking for help with their events."

I scoffed, shaking my head. "You want me to work with the nerds? That's not going to happen." I ran through the group of people he was talking about in my head, the ones who were always happy and talked about how much they loved school.

There was one, though, that stood out, her blond hair and blue eyes pulling me in every time I saw her. Kate Adams.

I pushed those thoughts away, knowing that even contemplating having a chance with her was going to be a disappointment. She was one of those people who was nice to everyone, always had a smile on her face, and was just about the complete opposite of myself.

Mr. McKee glared at me, his expression thoughtful for several seconds. "Do you want to stay here at Rosemont? Do you want to continue to play baseball?"

"Yes, sir." My stomach constricted, and it was like someone was squeezing my lungs because air couldn't go in or out. He was threatening me with baseball, the only thing I had to look forward to besides fixing cars at Doc's garage. The next words out of his mouth were not going to be good.

"Then you'll do this. Maybe a little school spirit, seeing the behind-the-scenes of what goes into the activities here, will help you remember that you want to be here." He paused, swiping at the corners of his mouth with his fingers before resuming his pose.

"I really don't want to kick you out of our school, Dax, but after all the fighting you've done since school started in

September, we need to fix this. Your grades are surprisingly decent, and I just don't want anyone to read your file and not understand where you're coming from." He glanced down at the papers for a few seconds, the silence tense with awkwardness. Who else would have their principal almost feel like a father figure?

Blowing out a breath, Mr. McKee nodded. "You'll work with Senior Committee for the rest of the year and you won't be in another fight—or else you'll be suspended, or expelled. And that won't go over well for your chances to play baseball in college."

College? I had to hold back a smirk. The Strattons had never been to college. Most had never even graduated high school, which was one of the reasons I was still here. I wasn't a quitter, and I was going to make it through this year. I just had to figure out how to control my temper in order to do so.

Mr. McKee wrote something on a paper and handed it to me. "Take that to your counselor so you can switch your schedule around. Fourth period is when the committee meets. I'll be talking to Ms. Schiels about this, and if I hear anything out of line from her, we'll have to take more serious action."

So I would be toeing a line for the foreseeable future. Not the thing I wanted to worry about for the rest of my senior year, but I should've thought of that before I hit Trent.

"What was Trent's punishment?" The curiosity was more than I could contain.

Mr. McKee glanced up at me with a no-nonsense expression. "I don't think you need to worry about him right now, do you? Worry about yourself so your grandmother can see you graduate."

And he went straight for the heart. My grandmother had secretly been counting down the days until graduation in the hopes that I would make it. She'd met the principal at one of our baseball games last spring, and they'd struck up an unlikely friendship.

I blew out a breath and stood, not sure whether or not I should thank him. I stepped out of the office and through the door before the secretary could turn and look my way. The bell had rung for classes, and since I had to change my schedule anyway, I decided to miss the first part of history and see my counselor. Maybe he'd let me get out of it altogether.

CHAPTER 3

KATE

I walked into Ms. Shiels's classroom, breathing out a sigh of relief as I glanced around the room at the bright colors and the different forms of art. She was the only art teacher at Rosemont and taught a wide variety of mediums. It had been in her classroom my sophomore year where I realized how much I loved creating things. Whether it was on a canvas or something digital, it was like my own safe haven.

Ms. Shiels was the one teacher I could be real with, who gave me grown-up advice and let me choose for myself what to do. She never made me feel bad for those choices, either.

"Kate," she said, glancing up from the desk. The bell rang, and the small group of students that made up Senior Committee chatted in the background as I walked up to her.

She held up a large poster, the design on it reminding me of the hours I'd spent creating it. We'd finally gone away from the traditional hay bales for Harvest, changing it to a glow-in-the-dark theme, and designing the banner had been so exciting. With the splash of colors across the black background, it looked even better printed out.

"You did an amazing job on this. Look at those skills you learned this summer," Ms. Shiels said, flattening out the poster on her desk once again. It had been tough getting my mother to agree to let me take a design class over the summer months, when I should have been using my time to pad my resume for applications to college. But this was something I loved more every time I sat down to try out. I just hadn't had the guts to tell my mom that yet.

I tried to hide a grin, the excitement bursting from me at her compliment. "Thank you. It looks even better than I thought it would."

Ms. Shiels lifted her arm, the bangles she wore daily jingling together as she used it to emphasize her words. "So, the printers just dropped these off, and then they should have the invitations all done by tomorrow afternoon. Which means we can begin selling them next Monday," she muttered to herself. A few seconds later, she stopped and said, "Let's discuss this as a committee."

I nodded and turned, taking the seat in the front right corner. When given the chance to choose a seat in any of my classes, I tried to pick the one closest to the door since I got called out often enough on SBO business. Less time disrupting whatever lesson we had at the time.

I loved being the student body president, getting to interact with all the students and do everything I could to make their experience in high school one to remember, but some aspects of it weren't so great, like having to plan a ton of stuff while trying to maintain my perfect GPA.

"Okay, class. Let's start the class period by getting these banners put up around the school." Ms. Shiels pointed to a small stack of posters in a box at the side of her desk. "Get a group of you to go into each section of the school. We need hallways in front of the school, east and west wings, as well as the locker rooms and gym. Don't forget to hang a few in the bathrooms, or as close to them as possible." She grinned at them. "Don't take too long. We need to discuss more about next week's dance, and I want to make some decisions by the end of the class period."

I ended up with Blair Castle and Cynthia Hart, the two who had just recently started dating, and they acted like they would die if they ever stopped touching one another. In some ways, they reminded me of a younger version of my mom and stepdad.

We, or I should say I, had hung up several posters on the second floor of the school when I heard a familiar voice call from down the hall.

"Kate!" My mother. She was probably just leaving some meeting with the principal or someone else in the administration. As head of the PTA, she made it her business to know everything about everything that went on at Rosemont High, making it so I couldn't make a move without her finding out a half-second later. I loved her, but there was a reason I was checking out colleges hours away from home.

I turned and forced a smile. "Hey, Mom."

The lovey-dovey couple took that opportunity to race for the art room, leaving me alone as I taped up the last poster.

"You've got everything you need for the dance, right?" She turned to look at the poster on the wall I'd just hung up. "Oh, those turned out nice. I can't believe how well you've picked up that designing program."

As much as I tried to stop it, my cheeks heated even more than after Ms. Shiels's compliment, and pride surged within me. It wasn't often I got compliments from my mom, but as overbearing as she was, she was getting better all the time. Her saying that made all the frustration to design the poster worth it.

"Thanks. I'm pretty proud of it. As for the dance, we're meeting right after we hang posters to make some last decisions. Ms. Shiels wants everything planned out by the end of the period so we can be prepared for the dance next week." I leaned against the railing that looked out over the commons area, the large section of carpet where most of the students sat for lunch or while waiting for school to start in the mornings.

My mother tilted her head to the side. "Any luck on asking someone to the dance yet? It's girl's choice, right?"

"No, I haven't had time to even think about it." That was half true. I'd thought about it a lot. I'd been asked to homecoming by Layne Ryan, who was super sweet and one of the guys I'd known since kindergarten, but there was something about it that made me not as excited as I usually was about dressing up and heading for a night out.

Masked Guy.

I had to be crazy to still be thinking about someone who'd kissed me six months ago. Even after a ton of secret research, I hadn't been able to figure out who he was. They say people can't recognize superheroes with masks on, and I kind of got it now. The only thing that had been visible was the guy's mouth and his crazy dark-brown eyes. Obviously, he didn't actually go to this school or I would have recognized him by now, right?

"I'll ask someone this weekend. It's not a formal dance, so it's not like I need to make reservations or anything."

She gave me a slight smile. "I saw Trent Jacobs in the hall earlier. He's such a kind, polite kid."

I frowned. Trent Jacobs was not the angel she thought him to be. "I think he got into a fight earlier, Mom."

I watched as her face fell for a moment, and then she tossed her light-brown hair over her shoulder. "I'm sure it wasn't his fault." She glanced down at her watch and then back up at me with a sugary-sweet smile. "Remember, this is the best time of your life." She took a few steps back and said,

"I've got to run and pick up your brother for a doctor's appointment. And make sure to get your math assignments done when you get home tonight. We've got to get that grade up if you want a chance at Stanford or Harvard next year."

She hurried off, and I cringed, shaking my head. Karla Adams-Pikowske would do just about anything for her children, especially to support Zane and me, ever since my dad passed away eight years before. My stepdad was pretty chill, but sometimes I wished the two of them wouldn't hover over us so much. I just needed some breathing room. And the chance to pick the college of my choice.

But I guess that would have to wait until the end of the year.

I walked into Ms. Shiels's class and settled into my desk, pulling out a notebook from my backpack. I jotted down the notes from the board in small, neat penmanship, concentrating on what I could help with in the discussion.

"We should be good as far as the refreshments for the dance. We've gone over the decorations, but we still need a DJ. The one we booked will be out of town for some big event down south." Ms. Shiels glanced over the room of about fifteen students, the pause meaning she was waiting for suggestions even though she hadn't asked a question.

The door creaked open, and there stood Dax Stratton, a cute guy who played baseball with my friends' boyfriends. I'd talked to him a couple of times, always in a group, and he seemed nice. A little awkward, but nice. For some reason, every time I came near him, his eyes got huge and he stiffened. Serena's boyfriend, Ben, did the same thing with most girls, so I figured Dax had the same problem.

"Mr. Stratton. What brings you to Senior Committee?" Ms. Shiels asked, reaching out for the paper Dax handed her, her tone revealing the tiredness I could now see around her eyes. She read through whatever was written on the paper before turning to look at him, a confused expression on her face. "Mr. McKee sent you?"

Dax nodded, keeping his eyes focused on Ms. Shiels's desk covered in art assignments from her various classes. "Yes. I'm supposed to be in this class for the rest of the year, I guess."

Ms. Shiels frowned for a few seconds and then said, "Okay, then. Make yourself comfortable in one of the desks. We're discussing the Harvest dance for a week from Saturday. You don't, by chance, know of anyone who can DJ, do you?"

Dax shook his head and stepped toward one of the open desks on the front row. He sat down next to me, and a smell of cologne or aftershave reached my nose. He folded his arms and leaned back. "No, ma'am. I only know athletes."

Of course he would be a little arrogant when it came to talking with a crowd. At least he'd added the ma'am in there. He'd been that way on a few occasions, acting like he was too good for the world, but when he turned in my direction, the same shocked expression and tenseness of his upper body made me have to stifle a laugh.

Ms. Shiels continued going over the items, and I glanced at Dax's face from time to time, whose body was as stiff as a board—well, as much as was possible sitting in a desk.

I leaned over and whispered, "What got you sent here?"

Dax turned to me and sucked in a deep breath. "Um, I, uh, got in a fight earlier today." His cheeks turned red past the dark stubble on his cheeks.

"The one with Trent Jacobs? That guy is a jerk. He probably deserved it." I shouldn't have been surprised as I'd heard Dax had been in another fight already this year.

All the times I'd spoken to him, I hadn't realized how built he was in his upper body, not until I'd noticed him during the fight. I leaned over, using my thumb and forefinger to shift his chin toward me. The stubble tickled my skin, but a small tingle flowed through me as I glanced up at his face. A dark bruise had already formed on the side of his jaw. "That looks like it hurts."

"It's not too bad," he said, without the arrogance this time. He lifted his hand to rub at it, barely brushing my fingers with his before dropping his hand like he'd touched fire.

This was a new punishment for Mr. McKee to dish out, but in this case, it might even be a good one. I'd heard about Dax's struggles with his temper from Jake. But there was something there, something behind his eyes that told me his life was very different from mine and that a little slack would go a long way.

"Rough punishment, huh?"

Dax's lips cracked a smile, and he whispered, "You're telling me."

We both turned and listened to Ms. Shiels, but every once in a while, I would glance over, more and more curious about Dax's background. My mother's question about who I would ask to the dance popped into my head, and I knew he was the one. My mother would be furious, with his less-than-crisp dress and arrogance, but it wasn't like it was a formal dance. And hanging out with someone different than my norm might actually make the dance fun this time.

CHAPTER 4

DAX

"What are you doing coming from that way?" Jake asked me as I walked up to the group of guys.

"I thought you had math down the other hall," Colt said, raising his eyebrows.

I shrugged and shook my head. "Principal McKee made me change my schedule."

Nate scoffed. "Right. Like the principal would even care about your classes." He paused a few seconds, and his eyes popped open. "You got in the fight right before fourth period? Dax, we leave you for five seconds and you get into a fight? You're going to get suspended or expelled, and then where would we be? We need you to take state this year." He leaned over and punched me in the shoulder.

"Thanks for worrying about yourself rather than my life, Dad," I said, feigning a frown. I waited several seconds before flashing them a smile. Seeing the relief on their faces was what I needed after such a long day.

Jake stepped forward, turning my chin, and the other eyes narrowed in on it. "Look at that shiner." He whistled.

I pulled my phone out, turning on the camera to see. A deep blue and purple bruise about two inches around covered my jawline and down into a section of my neck.

Seeing it reminded me of Kate's fingers on my chin. I could try to deny I had feelings for the girl, especially since I had zero chance of ever dating her. We were black and white, peanut butter and pickles. But for some reason, I couldn't put her out of my mind.

I growled, hoping Trent's punishment was worse than mine. "Yeah, it was me. My punishment is to be on the lame Senior Committee. I have to help them with the dance next week. It's a load of crap if you ask me."

Ben must have caught what I said because his voice came over my shoulder, causing me to jump back a bit. "Sounds like you got the best deal there is in high school after a fight. Decorating a gym or cleaning up trash? I'd take dance stuff any day."

"I can't even picture you in a fight, Ben," I said with a chuckle. He was the most chill guy I'd ever met, except when he took the mound in one of our games. Then he was laser-focused and determined to win.

Penny stepped up next to Jake, intertwining her fingers with his. I was both disgusted and jealous every time I saw them together. Not because I liked Penny, but because I secretly wanted to have a girlfriend. If any of the guys found that out, I'd never live it down. After Jake got together with Penny, I'd been dubbed the playboy of our group since he'd had the title before.

The thing was, I'd only kissed three girls ever, and the one I cared about was standing across the commons talking to someone. It was like my eyes were a magnet for finding her, even in the mass of students.

"Kate!" Penny called, waving to her.

I jumped and turned to look at my friends in the hopes

that they didn't catch me staring at her. Since they weren't paying attention, I glanced back over for a few seconds, her gorgeous smile making me wonder how I was going to survive the rest of the year in a smaller class where she was.

She walked over to us, still smiling as she took in the group. "Long time no see," she said to me, reaching out a hand and touching my upper arm for a second before dropping it to her side.

My cheeks heated, and I turned enough to avoid looking at my friends. "Yeah, a whole five minutes." It came out more gruff than I'd planned, but I was trying not to flirt. Flirting would lead to hope, and I couldn't do that.

"I need to head out," Nate said, taking a step away from the group. We all followed, walking down the hallway past the cafeteria.

"What's so important, Nate?" Ben asked, chuckling. Nate was usually the last one to have to go anywhere.

Nate groaned, turning up his nose in disgust. "I have to help with some campaign thing my dad has going on for tonight."

"I thought you weren't into politics," I teased. Nate's dad was the mayor of our small town, Pecan Flatts, and elections were coming up again in November.

"I'm not, but I don't say that in front of Carl Everton. I'd be thrown out if that ever happened."

Jake slapped him with his free hand. "Yeah right. That would decrease popularity points." We all chuckled at that as we continued out the doors of the building.

"Hey, guys! Wait up!"

I turned to see Logan, one of our outfielders, running after us.

"What's up, man?" Jake asked as we walked a bit slower for him to catch up. It had been fun having Logan at school with us this year. He'd been a starting freshman on the baseball team last spring and had made some unbelievable catches in the field. And even though he was only a sophomore, we didn't mind having him around. He was a funny guy, always cracking jokes.

"Well, I didn't get lost today, so I think that's a pretty good sign that I'm going to survive high school," Logan said, wiping his hand across his forehead as though he'd just run a race.

The rest of us busted up laughing. Our school was pretty big, but it had been six weeks since school started, and the kid usually showed up late for everything because he kept getting turned around.

"What's everyone doing tonight? Want to hang out?" Colt asked, hitting a fist into his palm. He tended to do that with a baseball and his glove often enough that it was transferring over into everyday life.

After murmurs of homework and other things, I finally said, "Gotta work. Maybe this weekend, though."

"Yeah, me too," Ben said.

"I've missed the last two days I was scheduled, so I can't miss this time," Jake said. He'd gotten a new job that summer at one of the car dealerships as a detailer. Once his punishment of working for Lou's diner for throwing Nate into a window was up, he'd hurried to find a new job—one that didn't consist of cleaning up people's half-eaten food.

They all veered off, and I stepped up to my heap of a car. It wasn't as nice as Jake's Jeep or Nate's Hummer, but it got me to the places I needed to be. I just needed to find some time when I wasn't working at Doc's garage and fix it up a bit. I'd bought it with my own money, which was the most satisfying thing in my life to this point. I'd been learning new skills for the past two years from the shop's owner, so I was sure I could do something to make it nicer. But using my time to earn money to pay for things usually trumped the looks of the car.

"Dax," Jake said after breaking off a conversation with Colt, "can I get a ride home? My mom dropped me off today since her car is in the shop."

I narrowed my eyes at him, wondering what it was he wanted to talk about. We were the closest out of our group of five, but we definitely didn't live close to each other. He lived in the middle-class area, not as nice as Nate's house but certainly better than the trailer park. What was he up to?

I shrugged and opened my door, sliding into the seat. The inside was humid, and I had to touch the steering wheel with the very tips of my fingers so the heat that had been beating down on it for the last six hours wouldn't burn my skin. It took two times turning the key in the ignition for the engine to start, and I knew I'd have to look under the hood after work.

I used the handle to roll down the window, and Jake did the same, though there wasn't much difference in the air temperature.

I pulled onto the road and reached over to turn the music lower than I usually had it while driving by myself. There was something about blasting my favorite tunes that picked me up after a long day.

"What's up, man?" I asked, glancing over at Jake before focusing back on the road.

Jake's smile was a mixture of concern and satisfaction. "What happened today? Why'd you try to rearrange Jacobs's face?" Not many of the baseball players were fans of the lacrosse jerk.

I shook my head, not even wanting to go into it even though the kid's words had been on a loop almost the rest of the day. All but the time I'd spent talking to Kate.

"It was nothing, Jake. Just him running off his mouth again."

"What did he say?" Jake's tone was hard, and I knew there was no changing his mind on this one. He was protective of his friends, much like he was of his mom and sisters ever since his dad had moved out when the divorce process began.

Tears pricked at my eyes, and I paused a few seconds, regaining control before I said anything. "That my mom died so she wouldn't have to put up with us. That she was too ashamed to live in a trailer the rest of her life." I swallowed hard, the rock in my throat causing a burning sensation to travel up to my nose.

Jake set his hand on my right shoulder, and I glanced over as I pulled to a stop at the red light. "You know that's not true, Dax."

I nodded, unable to speak. Grace Stratton had originally been a Claremont, an affluent family just outside our small town of Pecan Flatts. When she'd married my dad, her family had disowned her, but she'd never talked about being ashamed or regretting her decision, at least not when I was around.

"Your mom got sick. It had nothing to do with you, Karsten, or Bree."

The mention of my younger brother and sister brought me around. I'd been doing everything I could to protect them since she died the year before. My dad had taken her death the hardest, and it was getting to the point where I didn't even recognize him anymore. That was one of the many similarities I shared with Jake. Our dads were both alcoholics, and on occasion, they would take a swing or two at us. We'd become the masters of hiding bruises and cuts. Well, not Jake so much anymore since he didn't go on his visitation visits.

"I know. It's just hard to have that smug punk say things like that. At least he plays for the worst team we have at Rosemont." I laughed, the slight making me feel a little better even though Trent wasn't here. Rosemont Lacrosse hadn't won a game for the past five seasons, and it was a miracle the program still existed.

"I get that. Just, well, next time come vent to me about it, all right? Protect those hands, and your future. I know Nate was being funny about the whole state thing, but we won't make it without you, man. And I don't want to have to see you at another school."

"Agreed." I drove up his driveway and saw Penny just getting out of her car and leaning against it as she waited for Jake. "Really, man? You could have had your girlfriend drive you home. Now I'm going to be late for work."

Jake laughed and nodded. "Where's the fun in that?" His expression sobered. "I'm here for you, Dax. Whatever it is. Just let me know." He opened the door to the car and shifted out, dragging his backpack with him. He almost shut the door but stopped and leaned down, allowing me to see him. "Senior Committee, huh? Does that mean you get some more face time with Kate?"

"Shhh!" I hissed, glancing over to see if Penny had heard it. "You tell your girlfriend anything about this and we're done, man. I don't care how much you've got my back."

He nodded and tapped the top of my car. "No worries. That's one secret that's still in the vault. It's yours to tell, but Zorro needs to make his move soon or she might get snatched up by some other guy."

"Yeah, a guy like me doesn't have a chance with her. We're from completely different worlds." I hadn't known who Kate was until last year, but she lived in the same area of Rosemont as Nate and Serena. One look at my place would have her running away screaming.

"You never know," Jake said with a slight shrug and a devilish smile. "Maybe you'll charm her enough to be her boyfriend."

"Will you just—" I shook my head. Penny was walking up to us, and I'd punch him if he said another word.

"I got you," Jake said, looking behind him. He finally shut the door right before Penny leaned over and waved.

Studying those two, I just hoped my best friend would be able to keep my secret.

DAX

The drive home took a few extra minutes as I got stuck behind a passing train. I pulled into the small lot of trailers, parking behind my grandmother's old paint-peeling van. I blew out a breath, steeling myself for whatever I would find when I got in there. At least my dad wasn't home yet.

With two hands, I had to jerk the door open to get inside, making sure it didn't swing back to hit the trailer and ding it up any more than it already had. I hadn't had time to fix the door since school started. All my dad wanted to do when he got home was eat, drink, and watch TV, meaning all the little things that needed fixing were relegated to me.

"Dax! Dax! He's got my doll!" wailed Bree, my eight-year-old sister. She waved down at the other end of the hall where Karsten, my thirteen-year-old brother, stood waving the doll back and forth. I usually didn't care about their fights, but I saw the familiar brown hair and flowered dress and strode toward him.

"Karst, give it back. You know Mom made that."

He ducked out of sight, and I found him huddled behind

the door to my grandma's room. She was asleep on the bed, her heavy breathing turning into little snores. I grabbed the doll from him and pulled him out of the room, closing the door softly behind me.

In a harsh whisper, I said, "Can't you just leave her alone for two minutes?"

He glanced down, his jaw tense and the vein in his neck popping out a bit. "You're not Dad."

"I know, but use your head." I relaxed some and pulled him toward me, blowing out a breath so I could calm down. "How was school today? Do you have any homework?" I handed the doll to Bree.

"What happened to your face?" Karston asked, pointing to my jaw. Bree stepped closer to take a look too.

I opened my mouth, flinching as the pain from the bruise shot through the area. After only a few hours, I'd already forgotten about it. "I, uh, punched some kid at school." I glared at him and said, "But you better not do that. I'm already in more trouble than I can deal with."

After the fascination of the injury subsided, Bree shook her head and danced around with her doll in the air. "I don't have homework. We finished it all in class today."

I had to look away, the doll still bringing back a flood of memories of the time a year ago when Mom had made it for her, right before she died of breast cancer. If only things could have turned out differently. I wished she could have been there to mother us all instead of leaving me to be big brother and semi-parent during the times when my dad was on the road.

"I've got a little reading to do, but other than that, I'm all caught up," Karsten said, toeing the ripple in the carpet floor.

"Sounds good. Your grades are all good, right?" My words caught in my throat, and I tried not to worry about how weird it was to be asking the brother five years younger than me about his schoolwork.

He nodded, and Bree joined in. "Yup. We're good. I just need a signature on this one paper from Dad."

I took a step over to the cabinets and opened them, finding just a few packaged goods. "I have to head to work tonight, but can you make this for you and Bree, Karsten?" I held up a box of macaroni and cheese. "I think there's still some soup in the fridge you can warm up for Noni. Make sure she gets her medicine on time."

Karsten's nose scrunched in disgust. "Again?"

His response brought on the anxiety I'd felt over the last year, where I wasn't sure if we'd make it through another week together. There was so much pressure on my shoulders, and I didn't really have anyone I could vent to. Jake knew a little about my situation, but sharing it with any of the other guys was out of the question.

"Dad should be home tomorrow, and I promise I'll take you to the store and let you pick out what you want when he gives us the food money. Sound good?" I raised an eyebrow and waited for his answer.

"I'm getting cereal," Bree shouted, holding her doll up high in the air as she spun around in a circle.

I walked down to the small area where I had some drawers and changed into a shirt that I wouldn't worry about getting grease stains on. I grabbed my work hat and walked back to the door.

"Okay, get your homework done, and then you can watch a movie. Get to bed by eight thirty, and we'll do something fun tomorrow night, got it?" I pointed at each of them. "Mind Noni. Don't cause problems and help each other out, all right?"

When they both nodded, I headed out of the trailer and got back into my car. I sighed once inside, feeling the exhaustion creep into my upper body. There had to be more to life than just working and school. Just another reason I couldn't let Mr. McKee suspend me—baseball was an escape from real life.

I'd never been one to think about going to college, but I needed some way to escape this life, the constant lack of money and trying to keep my head above water. I needed to make some plans for my future because I wasn't going to stay in a trailer park for the rest of it.

CHAPTER 6

"You want to ask who to the dance?" Brynn asked over the phone.

"I was thinking about Dax Stratton. It would be fun to take him since he's good friends with Jake and Ben. And it's so last-minute that I'm not sure who else to ask." I stared at the ceiling in my bedroom, grateful for some quiet after a long day. To be honest, there were plenty of guys I could ask, but Dax intrigued me more than anyone else. And a part of me wanted to see why he acted funny around me. I'd asked Penny if he did that for everyone, and she told me that was not usually the case.

Brynn made a strange sound like she'd been hit in the stomach by something before she spoke again. "Last minute is waiting until next Friday night to ask someone. Still no luck with Masked Make-out Guy?"

"Brynn!" My voice screeched, and I paused, hoping my mother hadn't heard it. I dropped my voice down to just above a whisper and said, "I'm so over that. I've got so much going on right now that I can't even think about a relationship."

"Yeah, because your mom has your future picked out for you. What would happen if you got an A-?"

"Shhh! Don't even say that. I can't—like, my life would be over. It's just another reason why I'm in one AP class this semester. She's got me in so many extracurriculars that I might just die of exhaustion." I pulled a small section of hair and twirled it around my finger.

Brynn laughed and I joined in, thinking about how crazy that sounded, even though it really was my life. "I asked Garrett Park tonight. I dropped off a pizza with a paper inside the box that said, 'I know this is cheesy, but will you go to the dance with me?' His mom opened the door, so I'm curious to see what he says."

"I like it. Easy and done." My mind swirled with the options I'd come up with earlier. "I think I'm going to get a bunch of glow sticks and just say, 'Will you glow with me to the dance?'"

"That's a good idea. Then you won't have to buy as many for your outfit." She paused and then said, "Good luck. I can't wait to hear your mom complain about your choice in guys." Brynn laughed, and while I wanted to join her, her comment bugged me. It was true that my mom would flip once she found out I'd chosen someone who didn't dress like he was ready for prep school, but the fact that I'd been pushing off a relationship because of her suddenly fueled me.

We finished up the conversation, and I threw my phone on the pillows of my bed. It was still light out, but the sun was setting quickly, and I needed to get going if I wanted to ask Dax tonight. With my crazy schedule and the dance coming up, I just wanted to get the asking part figured out.

I'd gone to the dollar store and picked out several colors of glow sticks on my way home from school. Sure, there were plenty of ways to cleverly invite a guy to be my date to the dance, but to be honest, I was burned out. I'd been on some sort of class or student body committee since the beginning of middle school, and while dances didn't officially start until high school, I felt like I'd done every asking/answering idea out there. Penny and I had calculated that I'd only missed one dance in four years, and that was because I'd come down with pneumonia my sophomore year.

After a quick design of the tag tied around the sticks with a white piece of ribbon, I snuck it into my bag, doing everything I could to hide it from my mother. If she found out who I asked after the fact, she couldn't say anything about it or make me change my mind.

Dinner was a quick affair as she had a conference call with some of the other PTA board members and my stepdad had to finish up more work in his office.

My little brother had set up a snack center on the table in the family room, taking a few pieces of chocolate or gummy bears in between moves on his video game. My stepdad had put in speakers and other features to make it practically like a theater when we watched movies in there. Right then, it sounded like our house was about to be bombed with all the explosions in the game.

I swiped a handful of peanut M&Ms, popping a couple in my mouth as I sat down next to him. "Are you winning?"

He said nothing for a few seconds, punching the controller with his thumb harder and harder each time, shifting his upper body to the side as if that would help his character on the screen.

"I am now." He jumped up, pumping a fist in the air. "I just got the ultimate weapon. Do you see that?" He turned to me and pointed at the big screen.

I raised an eyebrow, trying to be as excited as he was. "Yep. That's good?"

Zane nodded, sitting back down. He was back to punching buttons.

"Zane, I'm going to ask someone to Harvest. Want to come with me?"

He turned and looked at me like I'd just proposed the most ridiculous thing ever to him. "You want me to go with you?"

I frowned, confused as to why he'd said it like that. "What are you talking about? It's been forever since we've hung out. Come with me."

He sighed and then frowned at me. "What am I talking about? You've got a bajillion things going on all the time. You're the Phantom of this house lately." He paused, laughing at my pouty lip and fluttering eyelashes in an attempt to sway him. "All right; I'll go."

We both stood and walked over to the door. He slipped on his shoes, and I sighed, steering him toward the door. "I'm sorry, little bro. Senior life and SBO stuff have me going crazy. But you can always come talk to me. Just ask."

He smiled, his eyes nearly disappearing with the action. "Done."

We got in my crossover SUV and strapped our seatbelts before I backed out of the driveway.

"Who are you asking to the dance?" he asked.

While we went to the same school, I wasn't sure how well Zane knew some of the older kids since he was just a freshman. "His name is Dax. He's a baseball player."

I focused on the drive, and the more I thought about Dax, the more excited I got about hanging out with him at the dance—if he said yes, anyway. I could already tell there was more to him than what was on the surface. He seemed different from some of the other guys I knew from school, and I could use a change of pace. Sometimes it got old having people tell you what you wanted to hear, and I'd been doing that all too often myself.

Besides, my mom would freak when she found out. Definitely a plus.

"Isn't he the one who gets into all the fights?" So it seemed Dax's reputation was more well-known than I thought.

I nodded my head and gave him a small smile. "I just think he could use something fun, you know? Maybe having someone listen to him will help change things a bit."

Zane leaned his head against the headrest and chuckled. "Of course, Kate Adams has to be the one to fix everything. What if he doesn't want to be fixed?"

A surge of irritation blossomed in my chest, and I bit the inside of my cheek for a few seconds while I breathed in, hoping it would help me calm down.

"I'm not trying to fix him. I just think some people could use a little more help in understanding what they want and need."

"As much as you say you're not like Mom, you sound like her right now."

Why had I even asked him to come? I glanced down at the map on my phone, finding we were almost to the address in the student handbook. It had been quite a while since I'd come out this far, and with how dark it was, I was surprised there weren't more streetlights.

I stopped on the side of the street when the directions said to turn into the trailer park. Part of me thought about turning the car around and asking someone closer to our house. The darkness of the area gave me the creeps. But then I thought about how Dax lived there every day.

I unbuckled my seat belt, turning to Zane. "Just stay here, okay? I'm going to run and drop this off, and we'll head home. Maybe we can grab a smoothie or something on our way back."

"Deal." He lifted his phone and started scrolling as I climbed out of the car.

I grabbed the small package from the bag in my back seat. With my phone in hand, I followed the directions since it was difficult to see all the house numbers in the dim light.

I'd almost made it when headlights flashed behind me. I placed the package on the small set of stairs and turned around to see that the car had parked right next to the trailer I was by. And out of the car stepped Dax Stratton.

He froze when he saw me. "Kate? What are you doing here?" He took a few hesitant steps in the direction of the door.

"I, uh, I." Why was my brain having such a hard time thinking of what to say?

For one thing, I'd never been caught delivering a dance invite, and I was making it more awkward than it needed to be. And then Dax took a couple more steps toward me, the head-lights backlighting him for a few seconds before they clicked off. The difference in the light showed off the strong cut of his jaw, and his upper body was a lot stronger than I'd thought. He was attractive, maybe more so with a line of grease from working on cars across his cheek. Penny had mentioned that was his job once when I asked about who fixed her car.

Finally gaining the courage to speak, I said, "I wanted to ask you to the Harvest dance. I thought it would be fun to go together." I sidestepped back to the porch and picked up the glow-stick bundle.

He waved at the trailer behind me and asked, "Are you sure you still want to?"

"What do you mean?" I placed a hand on my hip, trying to put together whatever puzzle he was referring to.

"After seeing where I live, where I come from, are you sure you want me to be your date?" His voice had an edge to it, but as I took a few steps in his direction, I noticed the vulnerability in his eyes.

"Why would this matter?" I motioned to the trailer and then looked back at him. "It's just a dance, and I think it would be fun." I closed the distance between us to hold the bundle out to him. His expression was wary, his eyes narrowed as he studied my face. Was he usually so skeptical?

As he took the package, our fingers brushed slightly, sending a zing of electricity up my arm. When his eyes scanned over the words, he smirked.

He looked up at me. "Your mom probably won't like it, but I guess I could go to a dance." He shrugged one shoulder and plastered on a smile that seemed foreign to him, making him look more arrogant than the Dax I'd seen several times before.

"You're not going to think of some way to reply?" I asked, taking a step back. Why I thought he'd play along and answer in the normal creative way was a mistake on my part. This night had definitely not gone as planned.

One eyebrow crept up, and he said with a laugh, "I just did. Let me know what I have to wear or what we're doing." The arrogant smirk was gone, and he looked a little more nervous than I'd expected.

I nodded and turned to walk away, when a thought hit me. Turning back to him, I asked, "Have you ever been to a dance?"

"Nope." He didn't even pause to look at me as he walked into the trailer.

A senior who'd never been asked to a dance? That was strange in and of itself since there were a lot of rumors about the guy making out with girls all the time. But what did I know?

At least I had a date to the dance, one my mother wouldn't approve of and someone intriguing enough that he might keep me on my toes.

CHAPTER 7

DAX

I sank onto the small couch in the living room, still holding the roll of glow sticks Kate had given me. It was weird to think about actually going to a dance, and even worse to think about how I was going to keep hiding the fact that it had been me who'd kissed her at that party forever ago once I started spending more time with her.

Thoughts ran through my mind as I stared at the empty wall in the dark. Did she even remember it? Or was she so popular that it was just another kiss to Kate? I didn't need to have this worry pressing on my mind since I already had enough on my plate with taking care of my brother, sister, and grandma.

Kate had been the third girl I'd ever kissed. My first kiss was with Bethany Summers in eighth grade when she'd attacked me after a group meeting we'd had. Girl number two was a dare from Nate at the beginning of junior year. Most of the rumors about me being some bigshot player were lies I'd made up to avoid people looking too closely at my life. The only person who knew more of the real me was Jake, but there were still some secrets I kept to myself.

I tried to portray myself as the old Jake, the one who didn't care what people thought and the one to make out with every girl. Penny was good to change all that. In reality, I was more like Ben, a little awkward and shy around girls, but more because of my real life than any speech problems.

But then there was Kate.

She was the first girl I'd kissed because I wanted to, because I'd finally gotten up the guts. Since the first day of junior year when she'd sat on the other side of the room in history, twirling her blond hair around her fingers with a bright wide smile on her face, I'd held a torch for her. There was something about her that sparked all the attraction senses in me, and whenever I saw her in the halls, I had to pretend I didn't care.

Because when in the real world did a guy like me from the wrong side of the tracks have even the slightest chance at a girl who had it all: looks, personality, and the perfect life? What did I have to offer a girl like that besides callouses and grease?

A floorboard creaked, and I turned to glance over at the hallway, seeing a silhouette walk toward me. Bree sat and curled up next to me, her thumb in her mouth and the old doll in her other hand.

"Bree," I whispered. "What are you doing up? It's nine o'clock."

"I just wanted to say good night." She only removed her thumb long enough to say the words before it went right back in, the soft sound easing some of the tension in my upper back.

More footsteps came down the hall, and I looked up to see Karsten taking a blanket and wrapping it around himself before sitting down next to me.

"Everyone having trouble sleeping?" I asked, chuckling a bit.

"How was work?" Karsten asked, his voice deeper than normal and his eyes barely open.

I sighed and leaned forward, taking off my ball cap with one hand and scratching at my crown with the other. "It was good. I got to work on this specialty car, a Ferrari, cherry red. I wish you could have seen it." I paused, sobering some. "Doc said I'll be getting a raise soon. That should help with all the little fees coming up. You have soccer practice tomorrow, right?"

Karsten nodded, his chest rising and falling as he took in a deep breath. "We've got a scrimmage against the other team in our club." The dread in his voice made me want to both laugh and cry.

"You'll kill them just like you did the last time. How was Noni? Is she feeling okay?" I glanced between both my brother and sister, trying to gauge the truth of their words through their body language.

"She's not doing good, Dax," Bree said, sitting up and pulling her doll tighter against her side. "She threw up the medicine."

I nodded, knowing our grandmother had been going downhill for a while, and this bout of flu wasn't helping. Her doctor had said that the illness was aggravating her diabetes, but I couldn't think of her dying just yet. I needed to figure out a plan for what I would do with my siblings while I worked once that happened. My dad was only home about eight to ten days out of the month, meaning most of the parenting fell to me and my grandmother.

"We'll be fine. We're the Three Musketeers, and we stick together. Right?" I looked first at Bree and then over at Karsten, who both nodded with a small smile. "Okay, let's get to bed, and we'll go from there. One more day until the weekend. We'll have to do something fun to celebrate. Maybe the park or something?"

Bree perked up even more, nodding her head so quickly I thought she was going to pull a muscle. She leaned over and hugged my arm before scampering off down the dark hall again.

"I've tried looking for jobs to pay for soccer. No one will hire a thirteen-year-old, though." Karsten's words rang through the silence, and I bit the side of my cheek, focusing on the pain there rather than the fact that my siblings had to live like this. We'd had a normal upbringing until our mother's death, and now with my grandmother's health declining, it felt like when Mom died all over again.

Our father gave us money for food after each paycheck, but all the other fees for school and sports had to be figured out by the three of us. Money for clothing was hit-and-miss.

"I've got enough to cover your fees. Do any of my old cleats fit you? You said something about the ones you have hurting your feet."

"They do, but I can't move like I need to in high-top baseball cleats." The whine in his voice was slight, and although it would be easier to just reuse the cleats I'd grown out of a few years back, I knew what it was like to not have comfortable equipment. It was the reason I'd splurged on all my own catching gear when I first got a job at the garage.

I nodded, scooting forward. "Okay. I don't work until later tomorrow. We can go to the store first thing and get you some."

Karsten grinned, his large buckteeth showing through as he headed back to his bed.

My mind drifted back to Kate's package that lay face down on the ground. A thrill of excitement shot through me, as if giving a shot of hope that I wasn't destined to stay in this trailer park for the rest of my life. With a raise from Doc at the mechanic shop where I worked, it would help my family get through the fall, and I might be able to save enough for a decent Christmas for the three of us.

For a moment, I longed for the Christmases of the past, my mother doing everything she could to make the holiday special for us. My dad was a lot different back then, happier. Less alcohol and heartbreak.

Shaking my head, I knew I couldn't dwell on it too long. Forward. I had to keep pushing forward or we'd all drown.

Before I checked on the kids, I walked into my grand-mother's room in the back. Her breathing had turned raspy over the past few days, her cough rattling from deep in her chest, and she was hardly eating anything. Our neighbor had offered to check in on her while we were at school, but the bowl of broth sat on the small rickety nightstand next to the bed, still full.

"Noni?" I whispered, touching her shoulder. "Noni, can I get you anything?"

She opened her eyes and turned to look at me, her eyes clouded over. "No, Stanley. I don't want to go to the field today. I've got the mending and cooking to do." Her eyes closed again, and I heard a soft snore.

I closed the door softly and walked over to the master bedroom where Karsten and Bree slept when my father was gone. They were already asleep, their heavy breathing echoing through the small room.

I made my way back out to the bathroom and took a shower, taking extra time to get all the grease off. It took all the energy I had left to drape a sheet over the living room couch before I collapsed on it. Seeing the package again on the floor, I turned, resting my head on my hand as I read over it again.

I should have just told her no, that going to a dance with her would be a bad idea, getting my hopes up and all that.

But the other part of me said, "Why not?" It was senior year, and it was one night out.

I just had to keep telling myself that's all it was.

45

CHAPTER 8

KATE

Saturdays were always hectic for me, but the good thing was that most of the activities for school were only during the week, meaning I could focus on the other balls I was juggling in my life. I worked at a dance studio starting at seven in the morning until noon, when I went over to volunteer at the soup kitchen or the food bank or nursing home, depending on the day of the month.

I knew it was overkill, but as my mom always said, it would look good on my transcript and college applications, which was a major factor in why I continued to do it. The other was that I didn't want to let my mom down.

There were little decisions I made, like taking Dax to a dance, that were more spiteful than they should've been. But there were a lot, like what college I should go to or what to do to stand out from the other thousands of students who would apply, that I usually listened to her and did everything I could to make her happy.

Karla Adams-Shepherd deserved a little something good after all she'd been through.

I glanced at the full-length mirrors in the studio, waiting for my students to come in. Several wisps of hair floated around the sides of my head, and I worked to push them back. If Miss Michelle were to see even one hair out of place, I'd get a scolding, and that wasn't something I wanted this early in the morning.

"Laura, are you all ready?" I asked the girl looking at me between two slits for eyes. She wasn't a morning person at all, but by the time class was over, she was usually bouncing off the walls and chattering non-stop.

The first class I taught was a group of older girls, about eleven and twelve, who I always loved teaching. They were funny and usually talked a mile a minute before we got started. But then things got quiet when they had to concentrate on their hip-hop or salsa dancing, depending on the week. The next class made me want to just squeeze them all because at three, four, and five, they were the cutest little dancers in their ballet outfits.

I had a break after that class since one of the other girls my age taught it. Miss Michelle had run to pick up a few packages that had arrived for the studio at the post office, and the lobby was fairly quiet. I was sitting at the front desk, scrolling through my phone when I should have been figuring out my math homework.

The door opened, and I glanced up, seeing a girl about seven or eight walk in dressed in shorts and a t-shirt that looked almost too small for her. I smiled at her, ready to ask what I could help her with when a tall figure came through the door behind her.

"Dax? What are you doing here?" I still felt a little awkward after the exchange we'd had Thursday night, and I'd only seen him in the halls on Friday. I could talk to a lot of people, but I struggled talking to someone I'd asked to a dance until the night of the dance. Maybe it was so they wouldn't think I was crazy with all the stuff I had going on. I'd always teased Penny about being busy, but hers was with softball, work, and all the studying she did. Ever since this year hit, I really had become the Phantom in my house like Zane said.

Dax raised an eyebrow, looking uncertain as he stared at me. "I, um, well, my sister wants to take a dance class. I thought we'd come see what we needed to start her in it."

I switched my gaze from Dax to the young girl and grinned. "Awesome! We always love having new dancers here. What's your name?"

"Bree." Her voice was so soft that I had to wait a few seconds for my brain to process it.

"It's nice to meet you, Bree. I'm Kate, and I teach some of the classes here. How old are you?" I walked out from behind the desk and bent over, waiting for her response.

"Eight."

I nodded. "Sweet. Okay, we have a couple different classes we can put you in. Let me get you a calendar." I walked over to the wall where several fliers were kept, pulling out the one on lime-green paper.

As I handed the paper to Dax, our fingers brushed for a second, and a shock caused me to jerk my hand back.

"I'm sorry," Dax said, cringing. He held out his hands, stopping them a few inches from me, looking more worried than I would have with just a shock.

"I'm fine. Just too much static in this place, I guess." I grinned at him, and several seconds passed before I remembered what I was supposed to be doing, my heartbeat thundering in my ears. What was my problem? I didn't usually act this awkward around anyone, especially guys.

I turned so I was standing next to him, allowing me to see the paper at the same time. "Does she have any experience?"

Dax shook his head. "No, I don't know much about dance, so I haven't done much to get her started yet. She's been begging me the last few weeks, so I thought I'd check here first." He gave me a hesitant smile and shrugged.

"No worries. Here are a few of the classes we offer. We have some beginner ballet that would work for her, or several other options like tumbling, hip-hop, cheer, etc."

"Cheerleading!" Bree said, bouncing on her toes.

Dax frowned, his finger tracing over the sheet as he found the class she wanted and saw the time. "I'm sorry, Bree, but that's right when I work. I wouldn't be able to bring you to class. Ballet would work, though, or even the hip-hop on Tuesday nights." His voice sounded strained, like he was out of his element or just couldn't believe he was doing this. From his comment about knowing only athletes during Senior Committee the other day, I was surprised he was even here in the first place.

"I could pick her up if you want. I teach the cheer class for the younger group, and it wouldn't be a big deal."

Bree's grin couldn't be any wider, and she clasped her hands together, silently pleading with Dax.

He shook his head. "No, we can't do that to you. It's not like we live close enough to here that she could walk home after the class is over."

"That's the only class I teach on Thursdays, so it's not a problem," I said, giving him a small smile. I was surprising myself at how much I wanted him to say yes. Maybe it was my love of dance and cheer that made me want all little girls to have the chance to do it. Or maybe it was that I wanted to help Dax out.

"We just need a parent signature right here," I said, grabbing a paper with a clipboard and pen. "You can take this home if you want and bring it back."

Dax took the paper from me, looking over the sheet.

"Yeah, our dad just got back this morning, so we'll have him sign it and she can bring it in during the first class." He scanned the paper for something and then glanced at me. "What are the prices?"

"It's thirty-six dollars a month for one class at her age, and then it goes up for more classes." I watched as he mumbled something, his eyes going to the ceiling as he tried to figure out some invisible problem.

Blowing out a breath, he glanced down at Bree. "I think I can make that work, sis."

Bree jumped up and down like she'd never been more excited about anything in her life.

I tried to figure out what he meant by that. "You can pay with cash, check, or card. Just bring it with you, or you can pay now."

"I get paid this week, so I'll have to pay then." Dax's face was solemn, so different from the arrogance I saw from him before.

"Okay, sounds good." I turned to Bree. "I'll pick you up a little after school on Thursday. Are you excited?"

Bree nodded, leaning forward and wrapping her arms around my legs. "Thank you so much."

"Okay, just wear a white t-shirt and some black shorts to workouts. We haven't done fittings for the uniform yet, but that's scheduled for this week, so it's good timing."

Rubbing his face, Dax wiggled his jaw back and forth. "Sorry, but how much does the uniform cost?"

"I don't have exact numbers, but I think it's usually around two hundred."

Dax sucked in a breath and nodded, looking like that wasn't the answer he was hoping for. "Okay. That helps to know. Uh, well, I'll see you in school." He placed his hand on Bree's back and gently led her out of the studio. He quickly glanced back at me, and I smiled, more and more surprised by Dax each time I saw him.

Maybe he wasn't the bad boy everyone had labeled him as.

CHAPTER 9

"Cheerleading, huh?" I asked Bree as we got back in the car.

"I really want to learn how to do all the cool tricks they do, and Vanessa said she's in cheerleading and loves it. It sounds like so much fun, Dax." Bree took a long breath after spilling the words out.

I nodded. "We'll figure it out. Hopefully we don't have to pay for any competitions. That might be more than I can do right now."

Bree's face fell. "If it's too much, I can try something else." The sadness in her voice made my heart crack.

I reached across and rubbed my hand over her hair, causing her to duck out of the way and frown at me. "We'll be fine, Bree-bug."

As we drove home, I just hoped that raise would come through from Doc. I could use every little penny to help me pay for my baseball, soccer for Karsten, and dance for Bree.

* * *

Monday came faster than I expected, and I wasn't ready for a new week to start. My father had left early that morning, and it had been a relatively calm weekend with him home. He'd spent more on beer to last him the time he was there, but I'd learned better than to say anything about it. The bruise on my jaw from Trent was slowly healing, and I didn't need to go to school with a black eye to cause questions.

Fighting at school was one thing because everyone knew what the bruise was from. But getting hit by my father was more difficult to explain away. Plus, I didn't need a black eye to be immortalized in my first, and probably only, dance pictures.

I sat in math, listening to the teacher long enough to understand the problem, and then let my mind wander as the same kids asked a million questions about possibilities for the answer. I'd figured it out in less than ten seconds before turning my attention to the practice I had later. Fall baseball wasn't as intense as the regular season in spring and summer, but there were still some tournaments we had to travel to. At least I didn't have one until the week after the dance. Otherwise, I'd have to tell Kate I couldn't make it. My dad would be home again next weekend, and I hoped he'd be in a better mood.

Then again, if Noni kept getting worse...I didn't want to think about it.

I made it to lunch, not really excited for the rest of the day.

"We should just skip fourth period," Nate said as we walked out to our cars. "We could go to the diner or even my house. I think the pantry just got restocked."

"Yeah, that's the last thing we want to do," Ben said, shaking his head.

Jake chuckled. "Nate, did you forget that the last time we did that, you got a lecture from the mayor?"

Nate rolled his eyes. "Stop calling him that. He's my dad first. And the only reason he got mad was because someone…" he paused and stared in my direction, "ate his favorite chocolates."

I shrugged, knowing it was the truth. "What can I say? He's got good taste." Not to mention I'd eaten way more than I should have of a lot of other things in the house.

There was a pause as we turned to look at one another by the cars.

I shook my head. "If I miss fourth period, Mr. McKee will know. As much as I don't want to care what he thinks, he has the power to suspend me from baseball." And I secretly wanted to see Kate. I was the definition of a glutton for punishment.

A collective murmur of "Go to class" came from the rest of them. We grabbed a burger at a fast-food restaurant and headed back to the school.

Now it was time to see Kate again. I breathed in deeply, trying to work up to my usual arrogance mask. That was the easiest way to get people to think I was the bad boy and to just leave me alone, unless it was for some kind of punishment. It was easier to let her think that of me, because to see the glimmer of pity she'd shown me the day she'd pulled up to our house to ask me to the dance was something I didn't want to see ever again. At least she hadn't looked at me that way since.

I strolled into the classroom just as the bell rang, stopping just a few feet inside as I stared around at all the long rolls of butcher paper. With paint and brushes set out on each station, it looked like we were decorating posters for something today. Maybe I should have taken the chance to ditch out.

"Let's get started decorating the posters," Ms. Shiels said, waving to the paper spread out on desks and the floor. "We want to get them hung all over the school before the end of the period. Pair up and get started. We need some posters to cheer on the volleyball team, a couple for the football team, and several for the dance."

I glanced around the room, seeing that most of the students had already paired up and were dipping their brushes into the small tubs of paint. All but one student.

Kate looked up at me and smiled, waving me over. Of course, it would be her. It seemed like ever since I'd kissed her back in the spring, there was something that pulled her to me, but in the last few days, it was like the universe was pushing me to her, as if I needed to come clean about the kiss.

"Hey," she said, tucking a strand of hair behind her ear. "We're in charge of one of the football signs. You ready?"

I shook my head. "I'm not sure you want me doing anything on this poster. The best I can do is stick figures, and my handwriting is horrible." Just ask Mr. Kendall, my English teacher. He always complained about being unable to read my work."

She chuckled and used the brush to make a long blue stroke on the paper. The movement was so graceful that I was mesmerized as she dipped the brush to get more paint and continued with another one of the letters. Her handwriting was similar to the signs I'd seen throughout the years at Rosemont, the perfect letters with the swirly font that could've been from a printer.

"Wow, you're really good at this," I said, not thinking before I spoke. What happened to the tough-guy persona I'd planned on using to distance myself from her?

She laughed again, the sound a light tinkling in the air. "Well, I'd better be. I've only been making these posters for years."

"You've been an officer that long?"

With a nod, she said, "Yeah. My mom kind of forced me into it at first, but I've loved every minute of it. It's a lot of fun once you get elected, and I feel like I get to know more of the students this way."

I watched as she added some embellishments to the paper, and when she gestured for me to help, I took one of the brushes and pressed down, making a couple of dots here and there. That was the best I could do without ruining her hard work.

She held up the brush and took a step back, examining the paper. A small smile crossed her face.

Wow, she was pretty. I'd never really let myself look too long at the girls in school because I knew things wouldn't work out in the end, that most would just judge me for where I lived and my family situation. But the fact that she hadn't done that, that she still treated me the same even though she knew I lived in a trailer, made whatever feelings I'd had for her over the last few months grow even more.

"Too bad I didn't know you last year," I said, shaking my head. "You could have done my art assignments for me."

Her laugh came out as more of a snort, and she covered her mouth and nose, her eyes wide with horror. "That was ladylike." She walked over to another poster that was still blank and said, "Well, if only you were good at math and could just take that class for me."

"What math are you in?"

"Calculus. I don't think I was quite ready for that yet, but my, um, my mom said I needed to continue taking all the classes I could so it would prepare me for college. I'm just barely catching on to the trig stuff I had to learn from last year." Her lips pressed together, her cheeks rosy as though she'd shared too much.

I stuck a hand in my jeans pocket, giving her a one-shoulder shrug. "I could help you with it if you want. Math comes pretty easily to me."

She turned her head, unable to hide the surprise from her expression. "Really?"

"Yes, really. I know, everyone thinks I'm a screw-up, but I do have some redeeming qualities," I said, trying to give her a smoldering look but failing.

"I never said you didn't," she said, grinning up at me. The way she hadn't hesitated to say it caused tingles to travel up my spine.

We worked for several minutes before the posters were ready to be hung. As we left Ms. Shiels's room, I could smell a scent of vanilla coming from Kate and leaned a bit closer, hoping to catch another whiff. There was something about this girl that went against everything I'd ever learned about the popular girls. She wasn't into appearance as much as I'd always expected, given the fact that she'd asked me to the dance. And she didn't seem to have many troubles. Then again, that was just me on the outside looking in.

I liked this girl—had a crush on her since before our mystery kiss. I just had to keep my guard up. With my luck, I'd be the one to end up with a broken heart.

CHAPTER 10

I held out another long piece of tape, and Dax took it from me, our fingers touching for a second in the transition. His eyes locked onto mine, and for several seconds, I was buzzing with energy.

"Are you serious about helping me with math?" I asked to break the connection between us. I was beginning to feel things for Dax that I didn't have time for. So much of my life felt scripted that a hint of excitement ran through me at the thought that he would be spending more time with me if he helped me out.

"Of course. I just have to find a time. I work a lot when baseball isn't going on."

I tilted my head to the side and debated whether or not to ask him about it. "Where do you work?" It was a safe enough question.

"McGreevy's Garage. I've been working there since I was fifteen." He stepped down off the small ladder and picked it up, moving it to the other side of the paper we were hanging.

I was impressed. It wasn't something I'd figured a guy like him would have done, especially since he was so arrogant in bigger crowds. But glancing at his fingers, I could see a hint of black grease in his cuticles.

Before I could stop myself, my mouth kept asking questions, this one what I'd really wanted to ask since he'd come into the studio with his sister.

"How come your mom didn't come with your sister?"

From the look of pain slicing through his expression, I wanted to grab the words and swallow them back. He'd been nothing but nice to me, and here I was, asking very personal and painful questions.

"She, uh, passed away a year ago. My dad drives a truck, so he's on the road a lot. I do a lot of the shuttling of my brother and sister to their activities—when I'm not working, that is." He gave me a small smile and grabbed the corner of the poster before stepping up on the ladder.

"I'm so sorry. So, so sorry. I didn't know you'd lost her." My cheeks were on fire, and now would've been the perfect time to go hide somewhere far, far away. I was usually so under control, knowing when to push and when to stay silent, but it seemed like anytime I was around Dax, those senses were out of whack. Almost like I had to know the answers to my questions so I could figure out why I was starting to crush on him.

He shrugged and grabbed the piece of tape from me again, hanging the poster up against the light-brown brick of the commons area. I hurried and put a piece of tape on the lower corner and then stepped back, waiting for him to come back down.

"It's not a big deal now. Just my life, I guess." His voice was strangled at the end, and a shadow passed over his hand-some features.

I bit my upper lip as we walked down the few stairs and over to another spot where we would hang the other poster we'd made. Trying to think of something to say, I turned to him and smiled, handing him one end of the rolled-up poster to spread out.

"Well, if you need help picking out her dance attire, let me know. It's one of my favorite things."

Dax raised an eyebrow, and the corner of his mouth quirked up. "Picking out dance clothes? I thought she'd just need a cheerleading uniform?"

I laughed, shaking my head. "That's for competitions. Does she have a white t-shirt and black shorts? That's for the practices at the beginning."

He paused and then shook his head.

"Maybe you can help me with my math before or after we shop for your sister's stuff."

He nodded, setting the step ladder up against the wall where I pointed. We were near one of the entrances to the school. This time the brick was white.

"How about tomorrow afternoon?" I said when he didn't say anything.

"I have to work tomorrow. Can you do Wednesday? Then she'll have her stuff for the first class?" His expression was unsure, as if everything connected to dance was some great mystery and totally new ground. Then again, I was usually just as lost when it came to baseball. Thank goodness for Penny's advice and slight coaching for the games I had to attend during the school year.

"Wednesday will be perfect. We'll just need to go right after school. I have to be at one of my, well, a thing I have scheduled." For some reason, telling him I was volunteering at the soup kitchen with my mom sounded more conceited than I wanted to convey to him.

We finished hanging the posters and made our way back up to Ms. Shiels's classroom, not saying much on the way. It was the first time I didn't feel like I had to blab on and on to someone else, and I liked the peace of it.

When the bell rang, Dax stretched out a small piece of paper to me. "Here's this, just in case you need to change anything." He gave me a tight smile as I took it and unfolded the paper to find a phone number.

I grinned. "Thank you. Sometimes I run a few minutes late, but this will help in case something major happens. I'll see you then."

He turned and walked out the door, almost running away. I didn't mind watching him walk away, and the fact that he'd given me his phone number without some lame pick-up line said volumes about who he was underneath the façade.

But I couldn't let my heart gallop away too quickly. I was supposed to be focusing on colleges and working on all the little things that would pad my applications. A boy like him would only make things more difficult when it came to the end of the year.

CHAPTER 11

DAX

It had been hours since school let out, and my ears were still burning every time I thought about giving Kate my number at the end of class. Sure, I'd pretended I was suave and a ladies' man, but real life was quite the opposite. The way she'd taken it and smiled, staring up at me with those blue eyes, made my heart pump a little faster even now.

"What are you thinking about?" Bree asked, sitting on a stool next to me at the sink.

We'd just finished up dinner, the three of us kids and Noni, and it was my turn to do the dishes. I loved it when Noni had the energy to cook because her food tasted so much better than packaged meals. She'd started feeling better on Saturday night, and by the time I got home that afternoon, she already had a stack of dishes in the sink from cooking. She'd made her special ravioli for tonight, and I needed to write down her process to keep for the future.

My phone buzzed, and I wiped off my hands on a towel before slipping it out of my pocket. I tried to keep a smile from my face since Bree was staring at me so attentively, but I couldn't keep a completely straight face.

This is Kate. Just wanted you to have my number too.

I nodded and tucked the phone back into my pocket, not sure what to say just yet. The crush I had on Kate was only growing stronger, but sooner or later, I'd have to tell her I was the masked guy who'd kissed her at that party. If she didn't remember the kiss, I'd feel like the biggest idiot. If she did, would that turn her off? What had I been thinking anyway?

With a groan, I rinsed off a plate, wondering why my life couldn't have been a little simpler. I couldn't change where I lived or my family, but I dreaded the idea of her looking at me like I was some insane person who just kissed random girls at parties.

There's a football game we have to go to on Friday. Do you mind if I ride with you?

She wanted to go with me? Again, I was baffled at how much interest she'd taken in me recently. But to say I wasn't excited by the sudden attention would be a lie. I just hoped I wasn't a pet project to help her look good in front of the college admissions boards of the various schools around us.

Sure. I guess I better go. I almost mentioned that Mr. McKee would probably be taking note of whether I showed up or not, but I didn't want to ruin the moment. I didn't have to work Friday night and didn't have another excuse as to why I shouldn't go.

Awesome! Okay, we'll talk more about it.

A few seconds passed, and another message came through.

What are you doing right now? ;)

Dishes, I replied and set the phone on the counter. It wasn't some eloquent answer, but I was close to done with the rest of the chore and the suds had already disappeared. I dipped my hands in the cold water and pulled the plug, allowing the water to drain. It was easier to wash the pots with a scrub brush anyway.

When the phone buzzed again, Bree picked it up before I got the chance, my hands still wet from the water.

"Ooo, Dax. Is this your girlfriend?" She made a kissy face and laughed, her doll tucked beneath one arm.

I wiped my hands off on a towel and swiped at the phone, missing and nearly knocking her over. "She's not my girlfriend. She's just a friend from school."

Bree's lips moved as her finger scrolled on the screen. "Wait, is this the Kate from the dance studio?"

Clamping my mouth together in an attempt to show no emotion, I nodded.

"And the one who asked you to the Harvest dance?"

Letting my head fall back in exasperation, I said, "Yes, Bree. The same girl."

She grinned, a twinkle in her eye. "It sounds like she kind of likes you."

My pulse quickened as she said that, surprising me at how much I wanted that. Of course, what kind of guy wouldn't want to have the attention of one of the nicest and most outgoing girls in school, and beautiful to top it off? But that was just a wish, and I knew nothing could come of it. I'd seen her mother around the halls, and I definitely wasn't the type Mrs. Adams, or Shepherd, would appreciate having her daughter date.

I finally caught up to my sister and grabbed the phone from her, purposely moving to the bathroom. The one place in the trailer where I could actually read what Kate had sent me in peace.

I'd rather be doing that than trying to figure out these math problems.

I grinned. *What are you having a hard time with?*

It took a minute or two, but a frowny face came through and she texted, *Everything. The whole equation.*

I glanced down at the time on my phone, seeing it was only eight thirty. *I can meet you somewhere to help you out.*

What was my deal? I kept telling myself things would never work out between us, but there was something always pulling me back to her. For some reason, I wanted to make her happy, because if the person who always had a smile on her face during school functions wasn't happy, I guess it meant I wouldn't have a chance to be happy, or something like that.

A dialing tone sounded, and I saw her name pop up on the screen, asking to video chat. I pushed the green button, giving her a half-smile. "Trouble with math, huh?"

She gave me a feigned frown and then chuckled. "Are you in the bathroom?"

My cheeks heated, and I twisted my lips to the side, nodding. I dropped my voice a bit lower and said, "It's about the only place I can have a shred of privacy in this place."

I loved my dysfunctional family, but it seemed like I could never have something of my own, and right now I didn't want my siblings to say anything about my growing crush on the girl on my screen.

"I get that. My brother likes to barge into my room all the time. I still love him, though." She tucked a strand of hair behind her ear, glancing away for a moment. "Anyway, meeting you would probably be easier, but my mom would ground me until I was at least fifty for leaving this late at night. Any chance you can help me through here?"

I laughed at the way she said it, her voice going from sarcasm to a soft pleading. "Yep. I don't have much homework, so I can definitely help you for a few minutes."

As we talked about math, we chatted about other things.

It was easy to talk to her, to share the little things about my life, and I enjoyed hearing about hers.

I'd judged her before as someone who was nice to everyone because there wasn't some deeper part of her, but I'd been wrong. She was kind to people because she cared, and for the first time in my life, I realized how much I needed that.

CHAPTER 12

KATE

Working with Dax was a lot easier than I'd expected. He had such a simple way of explaining all the math equations that looked like ancient hieroglyphs in my brain. It shouldn't have surprised me that the guy who always got into fights wasn't just some low-level idiot, but under all the disguises he tried to throw up, he was actually pretty smart.

I'd been so excited to go shopping with him and his sister for her dance outfit, but I was disappointed when he said he had to take a shift at work because one of the other coworkers had called in sick.

"I'll still pick up Bree," I said at the end of the school day.

He ran a hand through his hair, sending a nervous glance in my direction. "You really don't have to do that."

I leaned forward and gave him a small shove in the shoulder, grinning at him. "I've been looking forward to it for the last two days. It's not often I get to help a girl pick out her first dance stuff. I don't have a sister, and shopping with my mom, well, let's just say that's more torture than fun."

He chuckled and shifted, stuffing his hand into his pants pocket. "Okay, then. I'll get some money out on the way home so she can take it with her."

I was struck by that, surprised by his admission. "Your dad doesn't give you money?"

His eyes went wide, making the whites more visible than normal. He shifted again, rubbing his hands over his face. "Um, he gives us some money, but I use a lot of what I earn for extracurriculars."

Jake called to us from the other end of the hall, and Dax looked relieved to see him. "What are you two up to?" His smile was wide, curious, as if he suspected something was going on between us. I leaned forward a bit, interested in what Dax would say.

My mind kept going back to the fact that he was going to pay for his sister's clothes and cheer class from what he'd earned himself. It threw me. Things had been tight for a while after my dad passed away, but I'd never had to pay for my own activities, let alone Zane's. Just another admirable quality in this so-called tough baseball player.

"Just talking about committee stuff," Dax said, his body stiff as a board. As his gaze darted between me and Jake, looking almost like a scared animal, I got the impression he didn't want me to say anything about his admission just moments before.

"Cool," Jake said, glancing at me for confirmation. "Ben said he'll throw batting practice to us tonight. You in?"

Frowning, Dax shook his head. "I wish, but I have to fill in for Cory at the garage. I'll have to head to the batting cages or something tomorrow before the game on Saturday."

Jake snapped and then they gave each other a side high-five that led into a weird bro hug, and I shifted to keep from laughing.

Once Jake walked down the hall and Dax turned back to me, he smiled and asked, "What are you laughing about?"

"You guys tend to have the weirdest ways of saying goodbye."

"Please. And girls don't?" His voice changed, going an octave higher. "Goodbye. Oh wait, I forgot to tell you a minute-by-minute replay of my day." He had to stop because he was laughing too hard to keep up the change in his voice.

I was laughing so much that I had to draw in long breaths. I reached out to steady myself, holding on to his arm. Wow, he was a lot stronger than I thought.

"Kate, what are you still doing here? Don't you have an appointment or something?"

I sighed. Mom.

I dropped my hand and turned. "Hi, Mom. I'm just thanking Dax for his help with math. Because of him, I got 100% on my pop quiz today." I turned and gave him an excited grin, melting a little at his surprised expression.

"Really?" Dax said, his voice a bit choked.

I nodded and turned back to my mom. "I think that's pretty awesome, don't you, Mom?"

Her lips were pinched together, her eyes giving Dax a once-over from top to bottom. A few awkward seconds later, she nodded. "Yeah, that's really great. Especially since you've been having a lot of trouble with math this year. You must be Dax Stratton, right?" She took a few forced steps forward, her hand extended toward Dax.

He nodded and shook her hand lightly. "Yes, ma'am." The way he dipped his head in sign of respect made my insides flutter.

"Thank you for helping my daughter. I have to run to another meeting, but don't be late for dinner tonight, Kate. We've got a lot to discuss about the school events coming up before Christmas." She waved goodbye, and I closed my eyes, blowing out a deep breath.

I opened them back up and turned toward Dax, whose eyes locked on mine, sending some kind of soothing energy through me. "Sorry about my mom. She can be a little…"

"Intense?" Dax finished, his eyebrow raised as he glanced in the direction she'd gone. Probably hoping she didn't pop out of the shadows.

"Yeah, she's been like this ever since my dad died." I glanced down at my feet, tracing the small style of the carpet.

His hand touched my bicep lightly, and I looked up, seeing the emotion playing on his face. "I'm so sorry. I had no idea you'd lost your father."

I shrugged. "Not too many do. He died in a car accident when I was nine. My mom remarried Bill about four years ago, and things have gotten a little better now that she doesn't have to work such long hours, but it seems her intensity is now in torturing me."

"I bet it's hard, but I'm sure she just wants you to know she's there and that she cares. I'd give anything to talk to my mom again." He gave me a small smile, and I felt even more guilt than I had when my mom first walked away.

"Great, now I feel like a jerk." I chewed on my bottom lip, hoping to fend off the surging emotions playing in my throat and eyes. It had been hard to lose my dad, but that felt like so long ago now that the feelings had been soothed somewhat, whereas Dax had just lost his mother a year ago. "I'm sorry."

Dax wrapped his arms around me and pulled me toward him. My five-foot height reached his lower chest, and if I hadn't been so sad, I might have found it funny. The fresh, clean smell of him only aided in helping me feel more comfortable, something I hadn't taken the time to enjoy with any other guy in school. Relationships had always been a no-

no with my mom. She said high school was a time to experience as much as I could, and then I could think about having a boyfriend once I got to college.

But the more time I spent with Dax, the more I wanted to be around him. His persona was completely different than I'd expected, especially since all the rumors I'd heard about him were that he was some arrogant baseball jerk who went out and hooked up with every girl around.

From what I'd seen of him, he was quite the opposite. He hadn't been a jerk to me and actually treated me like a gentleman would, something not many of the high school guys at Rosemont would do.

"I didn't mean it like that, Kate," Dax said, and I loved the way he said my name, really deep. "I just meant that families can get on our nerves, but we understand how much we need them once they're gone. I try to keep that in mind when my dad comes home on the weekends. Sometimes I think it would be easier for him to stay away, but he has his own issues. He lost the love of his life when my mother passed away."

I stepped back and smiled, wiping at a stray tear streaking down my cheek. "Thanks. Yeah, I get what you mean. Sometimes those experiences make it hard to see past their quirks."

"Are you okay?" he asked, using his thumb to wipe another tear. The care he showed only caused those butterflies to flap wildly in my stomach.

I shook my head and then nodded. "Yeah, sorry. I'll be good. Thanks for the chat." I tilted my head back and grinned at him. "I've got a date with your sister to the store after I run to an appointment at this, uh, service place." I hesitated, hoping he didn't hear that last part. "Good luck at work."

I walked down the hall, turning back as I got to the stairs.

He still stood there, his expression a mixture of confusion and happiness.

So many emotions played through me when it came to Dax. His reputation versus the guy he was in real life. Such a contrast that I hoped I wasn't starting to have feelings for the guy I'd heard about instead of the one I was coming to know.

CHAPTER 13

DAX

I walked back into the trailer after a long night of work, having had to stay late to help fix a special car Doc needed done for the customer to pick up early the next morning. He gave me a lot of freedom to work on things, but then again, he'd done a lot to train me over the years. And working on engines was something that came naturally to me, almost like math.

"Look at this, Dax!" Bree said, jumping up and down with a bunch of bags.

I laughed and then realized I hadn't come home to give Bree any money for the clothes. "Are those your dance clothes?" I asked as she pulled out a black piece of cloth.

"Yes, and a few other things. I'm so excited." Bree clapped her hands and giggled.

"How did you pay for them?" I scrubbed at my face with both hands, a pit forming in my stomach. I did everything I could to avoid being in debt to people, already knowing how it felt to mooch off others from before I had a job, and I didn't want my siblings to go through that.

Bree gave me a look to say I was the slowest person in the world. "Kate bought them. I told her I didn't have any money when she came to pick me up, and she insisted that we still go shop. She bought all the stuff in these bags, and even a couple new t-shirts I liked."

I slumped onto the couch. "Are there any receipts in there? I need to pay her back."

My sister peered into the bags and shook her head, her voice softer when she said, "No, she kept them in her wallet." Bree's bottom lip began to quiver, a sign that she'd be in a full-on meltdown if I didn't say something to stop it now.

I reached out and touched her arm. "Hey, you're okay. I'll just pay her back for it. I told her I was going to pull out some money for you to take, and I forgot on my way home."

Bree grinned, carefully folding the workout clothes and other everyday clothing and sliding it back into the bags. If there was someone who deserved to be spoiled with a shopping spree, it was Bree. She would keep everything in pristine condition for as long as possible.

I stepped outside and dialed Kate's number, waiting several rings until I was sure it was going to voicemail.

"Hey," she said, picking up, breathless.

"Hey," I said, surprised she'd answered. I must have taken too long to respond because she spoke first.

"How was work?" I heard her take a big gulp of air and smiled.

I leaned against the side of the trailer, tipping my head back to rest on it. After a long day, talking to her helped ease some of the tension that had piled on that day.

"It was good. I just got off a few minutes ago." I took in a deep breath, prepping myself for the total of the items Kate had bought my little sister. With all the fees for the three of us, plus new cleats for Karsten, it would be tight. If I had to pay her back in little amounts, I'd do that. "I need to pay you for the clothes. How much did it all come to?"

She giggled on the other line, and I pictured her small upturned nose scrunching with the sound. "Nothing. You owe me nothing. That was the most fun I've had in a long time."

"No, really," I said, pulling off my hat so I could itch near my forehead. "I want to pay you for all of it. Just let me know, and I'll get the money to you tomorrow."

"Dax, I'm serious. I wanted to do something nice for your sister. She totally deserves all the fun stuff. She's probably the sweetest girl I've ever met. Keep your money and let me have this." Her voice took on a harder tone, more stubborn.

I groaned. "Are you sure? I really didn't mean to forget to give her the money. I feel like such a jerk."

"You're not a jerk, Dax. I'm sure you can use the money for something else anyway." She paused a few moments, and I could hear her smiling by the pitch of her voice. "You're pretty special, Dax. Just remember that."

"Uhh…" I wasn't sure how to respond to a compliment like that. I'd always been the bad boy, the troublemaker, or the one who was destined for no good because of my family and where we lived. Then again, sometimes I played into that stereotype. Having someone say I was special made my head spin.

She laughed on the other end. "I actually have to go, but I'll see you at school tomorrow, right? You still don't have work Friday night for the game?"

"Um, no, I'm off. Yeah, I'll, uh, see you tomorrow."

She hung up, and I closed my eyes, wishing I could redo that last conversation. I'd always given Ben a hard time for struggling to talk to girls, and now I'd had a small dose of what he went through on a daily basis.

I wasn't a fan of being in people's debt because I already

got enough looks as it was. I didn't need to be burning bridges by taking advantage of people's kindness. It was something I would do different than what my father promoted.

But Kate had been so kind already. I just hoped that letting her buy Bree clothes wouldn't come back and bite.

CHAPTER 14

KATE

I brushed through my hair a couple of times before I threw on my officer sweater, glancing at the clock as I did so. Dax would be picking me up in a few minutes, and I was already more excited than I'd been to go with a guy in months. James had been a nice date for Homecoming, but he definitely didn't give me the same electric feeling I got every time I was with Dax.

The doorbell rang, and I raced down the stairs, hoping to get there before my mom opened the door.

"Hello, Dax. May I help you?" her voice rang out. Too late.

"Sorry, ma'am. I'm here to pick up Kate. We're going to the football game." Dax's voice came out monotone, and I bit my lower lip, attempting to hold back a laugh. He was so serious around her, and I wondered if it had anything to do with losing his mom.

"I'm right here, Mom. We'll be back as soon as the game ends." I hurried, hoping to shut the door before she said anything, but her foot stopped it.

She gave me a tense smile. "Why don't you take Zane with you? I'm sure he would love to go to the football game."

From somewhere behind her, my brother's voice called out, "I'm good. Football makes for a boring night."

I'd never been more grateful to my brother. I'd have to take him out for ice cream or whatever he wanted to do. Turning down my mother's offer was bold but also saved me the embarrassment of explaining everything to Dax, that my mom was picky about the people I hung out with.

She gave me a look that made me straighten up even though I hadn't done anything wrong.

"Dax is on Senior Committee with us, and we'll be with the rest of the officers in the student section," I said, trying to keep the exasperation from my voice. I was a people pleaser to the core, and having her mad at me would make the rest of the night uncomfortable as I worried about what she'd be thinking.

With a curt nod, she stepped back and shut the door. And that was why I still hadn't told her Dax would also be my date to the dance.

I turned to find Dax staring at me, studying my face. "Are you okay?" I asked.

He gave a little shoulder shrug with his hands tucked into his pants pockets, the mask of arrogance he wore the first time I really talked to him covering his face. "Are *you* okay?"

"What do you mean?" I asked, walking toward his car.

"Your mom clearly doesn't like me. If you want, I can just drive alone. Meet you there?" He gave me a strained smile as if trying to play off the fact that he wasn't okay with the whole situation.

I shook my head, opening the door for myself and sliding into the passenger seat. The feeling of letting my mom down niggled at my chest, but I wanted to be there with Dax, so I pushed it aside.

"Honestly, Dax, if I stopped hanging out with all the

people my mother didn't like, my group of friends wouldn't even exist."

He turned to look at me, trying to figure out if I was telling the truth or not. "Penny? Brynn?" He looked shocked just saying their names. He'd conveniently left out Serena, but that girl was her own person, and I loved that about her. She didn't worry about who did or didn't like her and her sometimes attitude.

I chuckled. "Yes, even Penny and Brynn. My mom has always seen them as competition, even though Brynn's only a junior. They're good students, and they're athletes. In my mom's book, that means they've already got a jump ahead of me in the college-application game."

Penny was the genius mind who studied all the time and took every advanced placement class offered at Rosemont, while also being the star pitcher for the softball team. Brynn was the younger equivalent, showing off her skills on the basketball court.

Dax stretched his back against the seat and shifted the car into first gear. "Wow, I know my dad isn't pushy about college, but comparing you to your friends? That's a little harsh."

I smiled politely, feeling guilty that I'd given him the wrong impression of my mom. In essence, he was right. But I'd gotten so used to her trying to control things that it almost felt normal, until other people pointed it out.

We made small talk as we drove to the high school, and I was surprised to see what a good driver Dax was and what a clean car he had. I didn't have to grab the "oh crap" handle once. So many things I was learning about the so-called bad boy.

We got out of the car and walked over to the stadium. Things hadn't filled up quite yet as we'd arrived much earlier than the start of the game to make sure we had everything in place.

"Do you have to do all this every game?" Dax asked, lifting a box of t-shirts we were supposed to sell for Senior Committee.

I motioned for him to set the box down on the table and pulled out a few of the shirts, arranging them on the table so that whoever worked it for the night had things organized.

"It varies from game to game. We're selling these shirts to help fund the senior gift." I pulled out several sweatshirts and set them up according to size next to the t-shirts. I'd learned to make things aesthetically pleasing from the times my mother had hammered it into my head or just by watching her get ready for events. To sell more, order was the best recipe.

"Senior gift? What's that?"

I turned to him, setting my hand on my hip and leaning on the table with the other. "How long have you been going to this school?" I asked, a slight tease to my voice. "The senior class usually gives a gift to the school when they graduate. We haven't decided on anything just yet, but there are graduating classes who donated the new scoreboard in the gym or the marquee outside the front of the school."

"Gotcha." He pulled out a couple more t-shirts, holding them for me to take.

Once that was all arranged, I walked over to the concessions booth. "Are you all set in here?" I asked. The smell of nachos and hot dogs drifted through the window, and my stomach grumbled, reminding me I hadn't eaten dinner.

Doris, one of my favorite people, was all decked out in her hairnet and apron, waving her plastic gloves in my direction. "We still need more utensils for the food. Do you mind grabbing some?"

I gave her a thumbs-up and waved for Dax to follow me.

"Where is the rest of the committee? Don't the other officers come early to help?" Dax asked, his long strides making it so I had to almost skip to keep up.

"They usually come a few minutes before game time. But I like to help out, so I come early to make sure everything is in place."

Dax laughed and shook his head. "You are one of a kind; that's for sure."

I turned, feigning shock with furrowed brows and my mouth open. "What do you mean?"

"I'm just saying that I do everything I can to avoid school, and here you are, spending extra time trying to get everything organized."

We both laughed at that, and I found his laugh to be relaxing, music to my soul.

"We just need to get this stuff, and then we'll head up to the stands. It looks like more students are filing in."

Dax circled his hands a few times and gave me a slight bow. "I'm at your service, Highness."

I slapped him lightly with my hand, again pleasantly surprised by the strength in his upper arm.

The guy was growing on me more and more, and my hopes to find the Masked Kisser had started to take a back seat, which I counted as a win. Serena would definitely be happy that I was starting to move on.

CHAPTER 15

DAX

It had been a while since I'd shown up to a football game. Usually playing baseball or working got in the way of it.

"Go, Logan! Run it all the way!" I cheered as the kid who played outfield in baseball was one of the starting wide receivers for our team. Some days I felt he had more speed than most of our team combined.

I watched Kate get excited about the game but then get distracted by all the people swirling around us. She knew just about everyone, and I was amazed at how she could treat everyone the same. The popular kids and the nerds were all equal in her book. But it still made me wonder why she was suddenly so interested in me. Maybe it was because she felt sorry for me and had decided to help me out with this new punishment I'd been given by Mr. McKee.

The thing that linked us together the most at this point was the death of one parent, and that amazing kiss we'd shared last spring. Had her sudden interest in me been because she found out I was the one to kiss her? I wanted to ask her about her kissing history in the hopes that it would come up and I could gauge my feelings compared to her reaction, but I was worried that would give me away.

Turning to her, I touched her arm and asked, "Do you want something? I'm going to get a drink at the concession stand."

She gave me that wide grin and shook her head. "No, I think I'm good for now."

I headed down the stairs of the stands and burrowed my way through the crowd. I raised my hand a few times when I heard people call out my name, but it was hard to find anyone with all the people around me. I finally made it past the stands and into a more open area, allowing me to breathe freely.

"One Coke, please," I said to the woman behind the counter. It was the same one Kate had spoken to before the game.

The woman nodded and took my money before filling up the cup. When she handed it to me, I leaned in, lowering my voice, and asked, "You know Kate pretty well?"

A smile spread quickly, the woman's expression lighting up. "Oh yes! She's an amazing young woman. Are you two dating?"

The question caught me off guard, and I shook my head. "I just joined Senior Committee, so I know her from there."

"She's just the nicest girl, though. I hope she finds someone who will treat her right. She's one of those people who make you feel good whenever you see her."

I thanked the woman and stepped back, sipping at my drink. She'd been right about one thing: Kate did make me feel good each time I saw her, which was different than most days lately.

"What brings you here?" a familiar voice asked from behind me.

I turned and laughed when I saw Nate and Colt behind me.

"Senior Committee brought me here," I said with sarcasm. "What about you guys?"

"We thought we'd come support Logan. He's been worried about this game all week, even though he looks like he's breaking records every time he steps onto the field. You doing anything after?"

"Probably just heading home. I've got work early tomorrow morning before the dance." I kept forgetting to ask Kate what the plans were. Seeing her before the game made me think she was so on top of things, but then again, she had a lot on her plate.

Nate glanced in the direction of the student section, and I turned around to look over at Kate. When I looked back at my friend, he gave me a mischievous grin.

"What's the story with you and Kate? Did you tell her about the kiss?" Nate leaned in, looking as though he couldn't wait to spread the gossip.

I gave him a firm punch to the shoulder and shook my head. "Did Jake tell you about that?" Hot anger hit my chest, and I wanted to punch something.

Colt chuckled. "We heard Penny and Serena talking about how Kate needed to get over the Masked Kisser, and we kind of put it together, bro."

I closed my eyes, wishing I hadn't stopped to talk to them. But the thought that she was still thinking about that kiss made me work to hide a smile as I said, "Nothing is going on between us. She's pretty much out of my league."

Colt shook his head. "I don't know. I've seen her check you out a few times just standing here."

I had to will myself not to look in her direction again, or that would give away my feelings for the girl—something I didn't need with Nate and Colt here. They would never let me live it down.

"We've done stuff together, but it's just been for the committee. Remember that if I don't participate, Mr. McKee will suspend me from baseball for the rest of the year." I watched as their expressions sobered. Good misdirection.

"Sounds like a benefit to me. Being forced to hang out with the girl you've been pining for over the past year has got to be awesome," Nate said with a grin.

I studied his eyes, and while I found a sliver of mischief there, he was rather sincere in his words. Had I really been that obvious?

"Yeah, it's probably better that you don't get into any more trouble," Colt said, slapping my chest with the back of his hand. "We don't need Wade to catch for us, or we'll lose every game this year."

I tried not to smile too wide about that, but it was the truth. We didn't have many catchers on the team, which is why I'd been starting varsity since my freshman year. The one who could take my place if something happened to me was a junior, and he struggled to hang on to anything that Ben Clark threw at him.

"I better get back to the group," I said, sipping my drink once more. I turned around, trying to be discreet at this point, and saw Kate glance in my direction. Her bright smile caused my heart rate to speed up, and I think it skipped a beat.

"Good luck," Colt said. "Maybe try and recreate that kiss again. See what she thinks of it." He waggled his eyebrows a few times.

I reached forward and nailed him in the shoulder with my fist, not holding anything back. My teammates knew me as a tough guy who didn't take crap from anyone, and even though I secretly wanted to kiss her, I couldn't let them get to me or I'd never hear the end of it.

"Leave it alone, Colt," I said, teeth gritted.

He reached up and rubbed where I'd hit him, his nose scrunched in pain. "All right, I will."

I turned and strode back to the stands, taking my spot next to Kate and trying to focus on the game rather than the memory of our first kiss swirling around in my mind. How was I ever going to keep working with her if I couldn't forget about it and just get through this punishment?

CHAPTER 16

KATE

The game was a lot of fun, and we won for the second time this season. Dax mentioned how the football team wasn't very good this year, but when the freshman and sophomores were seniors, the team might even have a chance at taking a state title. I liked talking to him about stuff like that. No one else in my life usually cared enough to explain the little things to me.

"Logan is our outfielder. He's also one of the wide receivers, which means he usually runs down the field and catches the ball from the quarterback." He had to lean into me to explain since the crowd was so loud, but I didn't mind. I was more attracted to him at the moment, as the mint-colored polo he wore accentuated the tan of his skin and the bulk of his arms.

As we spent time together, I found so many things buried deep, maturity being one of them. He was kind of an old soul, but around his friends, he did what he could to act like the typical egotistical playboy.

"Did you ever play football?" I asked on the drive back to my house.

Dax shook his head. "No. It wasn't one of the things I really cared about back then. I've always had a love for baseball. There are so many little details that go into it, and it fascinates me." He stopped talking, his body going stiff. When he spoke again, it was more of a gruff, macho tone than the sincere one from the sentence before. "I mean, who doesn't like slamming a baseball over the fence or throwing someone out on the bases."

I reached over and touched his forearm lightly. "Why do you do that?"

"What?" Dax turned to me for a second before glancing back at the road.

"Act like you aren't really smart? I mean, you get math way better than I do. Is that what you were talking about? Baseball has some mathematics or physics to it?" I waited, trying to convey that I wasn't going to judge him one way or the other if that's how he felt.

He blew out a deep breath, pushing his back deeper into his seat. "There are a lot of stereotypes about people like my family. Most people don't graduate high school or care about anything more than that. My father would laugh to the grave if I ever talked about how I like some of the subjects at school." He lowered his voice deeper, and it rumbled in my chest. "'We're Strattons, Daxton. There's no need for us to be thinking we can accomplish more than we can. We're stuck here, and if it's good enough for me, you'll be just fine where you are.'"

The look of sorrow on his face twisted my insides, and I reached forward, my fingers brushing the back of his hand that sat on the shifter. The warmth there soothed my cold fingers. "No, Dax. That's not good enough if you don't want it to be." How could a father suggest that?

"I've always wanted to be a mechanic, but I doubt I'd qualify for much more than a truck driver, like my dad." Dax spat out the last words, acting as though they would poison him.

I shook my head. "I'm not the poster child of living my own dreams…yet. Sometimes I think it's easier to just let my mother dictate things, and then I'll have freedom once I go off to college. But there are things I want to try out now, like learning to play the guitar, or even just going out with my friends without having a scheduled block of time on my planner."

"Has she always been like that?" Dax asked, turning into my driveway.

"No. It's gotten worse throughout the years. My stepdad has older children, and they are about as perfect as you can get when it comes to kids. Valedictorian, summa cum laude, scholarships, high-paying jobs. It's kind of hard to compare my life to theirs." I was on the high honor roll, but I'd never been focused enough to get a 4.0 every semester.

Dax shifted the car into park and turned to me. "Do you want to compare yourself to them?"

I blinked a few times, trying to process the question. I'd never thought about it that way. It was just how things were supposed to go in my life. "No. I would rather do my own thing, get a scholarship for my art or something like that. Majoring in business to go on to law school is not my first choice of things to do."

Dax chuckled, and I joined in, realizing how much my mother's opinions had taken over my life. I knew she was only trying to help, trying to do everything she could to set my life up for the future, but mistakes were normal for teenagers, and I should be allowed to make a few.

"Have you ever done anything you're not supposed to do?" Dax asked, that wide grin pulling me in.

I studied the lines of his face, the strong jaw, and piercing eyes. The attraction grew inside me, and I flicked my gaze to his lips, wondering what they would feel like on my own.

Then the weight of the question hit me, and I looked away. "If I have, it's been a while. Probably before my dad died." My stomach rumbled, again reminding me I hadn't eaten since lunch. I should have let Dax get me something from the concession stand, but I didn't want him thinking I was taking advantage of him.

Dax grinned, turning on the blinker and moving into the next lane right before the light to head in the direction of my house. The street he turned down led back out to one of the main streets.

I held on as he sped down the road. "Wait, what are you doing?" I looked around as the scenery passed then back at him, wondering what he was thinking.

He slowed down and parked next to the curb at the end of the street. "Your stomach has been growling for the past two hours."

"True." My gaze flicked to the dashboard, and I saw ten o'clock was creeping even closer. I looked back at him and paused, waiting to see what he said.

"We could go get a shake or something. No law-breaking, just an after-football treat." He gave me a close-lipped smile, and the internal battle of being home and responsible or staying out a little later warred.

"A shake sounds good." The words were small and high, almost squeaky. I was so used to following the rules to the letter that a slight terror filled me that I wouldn't be home right at curfew.

Dax must have sensed that because he said, "Are you sure? I can always take you back to your house if you want."

I took a deep breath, relaxing the muscles in my back as I released it. "No, it will be good. Like you said, we're not breaking things." Except for curfew.

He gave me a long look, staring into my eyes for several long seconds before he drove off. I didn't say much until we pulled into Lou's Diner.

We strolled in, and Penny waved, delivering several menus to another table. One of the other waitresses seated us, and a minute or two later, Penny walked up with two waters, her small notebook and pen in hand.

"Hey, you two. It's good to see you in here," she said, grinning. She turned a bit and winked at me.

Of course she would be excited we were here together. She'd been trying to match us up with all the baseball guys since she and Jake had started dating last spring. Serena had been the unexpected one to fall first.

As I glanced across the table at Dax, I could picture us together. Scratch that, I was in deeper than I should be.

"Penny, working on a Friday night, huh?" Dax asked, glancing over the menu. "Where's Jake?"

"He had something with his mom and sisters. I was supposed to go, but they needed a quick sub for tonight here. Money helps pay for college." She struck her waitress pose, a slight lean into the table, her pen poised above her pad.

"Scholarships do that too," I said, infusing my voice with teasing. Penny had always been worried that she wouldn't be good enough to get a scholarship for softball, but she'd already had more offers than the number of applications I'd submitted.

Penny shook her head, waving her hand in the air like she was waving the thought away. "Okay, what can I get you two?"

"I'll have a strawberry shake," I said, tapping my purse to make sure I had my wallet. I'd lost it one time a couple weeks ago and had to try and pay with the coins in my purse. I didn't want to repeat that in front of Dax.

"I'm going to go with a brownie sundae, extra whipped

cream." Dax took my menu and stacked it on top of his before handing the two of them to Penny.

My friend nodded. "Awesome. I'll get those right out." She took a step and paused, turning back to us. "How was the football game? You did go, right?"

I looked at Dax and saw he was waiting for me to respond. I kept my eyes on him as I spoke to her, seeing the small flicker of emotions crossing his face. "It was good. Dax taught me about a few of the positions and what they're supposed to do on the field. We won." I gave an exaggerated smile.

She giggled. "That's good. Rosemont Football can always use another win." With that, she walked over to the kitchen, disappearing around a wall.

Once she left, nerves took over my stomach, but instead of worrying about missing curfew, I found myself more anxious about being around Dax in a setting like this. It was almost like, well, almost a date.

"What's the plan for the dance tomorrow?" Dax asked, wrapping the paper from the straw to his water around his pointer finger. He looked a mixture of nerves and was trying to make conversation to combat it.

"Great question. I probably should have told you sooner, but I'm good at procrastination with the things that are actually in my control." He laughed at that, and I wanted to remember it forever. His casual sitting pose, the slight smile on his face making him look more tired than anything. "We're going to a rock-climbing place for the day activity."

He nodded. "Rock climbing, huh? I don't think I've ever done that one before."

"It's fun. I've been once. You should have no problem with those guns, though," I said, pointing to his arms. And then the realization of what I'd said hit me, and I was sure my face would melt off from embarrassment.

Dax leaned forward, the corner of his lips quirked up at one side. "You think I have guns?" His voice emphasized the last word a little longer than normal, and I could tell he was getting a kick out of this.

"Oh, please." I waved my hand in front of my face and shook my head. I was not going to keep embarrassing myself like this. "We'll have dinner at my house after and then head to the dance."

"What are we wearing? Isn't this one of the dress-up dances?" He leaned over and took a long draw from the water glass.

I nodded. "Yes, it is one of those. I've been trying to decide if we should go as Sleeping Beauty and Prince, or if we should do something Shakespeareish."

"Say what now?" He had to pound on his chest as he started to cough, water getting trapped in his throat. His eyes watered as he coughed a couple more times, and then he glanced up, waiting for me to say something.

It took everything in me to keep a straight face for at least ten seconds, and then I broke, laughing hard enough that I started coughing. When I got it under control, I said, "I wish I'd taken a picture of your face just then."

Dax studied me. "Why? Please say we don't have to dress up in old-timey clothing." He clapped his hands together and scrunched his face in a silent plea.

"It's a glow-in-the-dark theme. We can either go with white t-shirts or do all black and attach the glow sticks to our clothes."

I sat back as Penny approached with our order.

"Here's your shake and your sundae. Can I get you guys anything else?" Penny asked.

Dax took a scoop of the brownie-and-ice-cream combination and shook his head. "No, this is delicious."

I took a bite of my shake, savoring the bits of strawberry. "What are you and Jake wearing tomorrow, Pen?"

"White shirts. Jeans. Light-colored shoes." She shrugged, dropping the tray she'd brought our desserts on by her side.

"I just can't believe you've gotten him to go to all these dances," Dax said in between bites.

"You and me both, Daxy. It's always a little touchy, but he didn't protest much this time. It's fun to have something to go to." She glanced down at the table, probably trying to see if there was anything else we needed. "What about you two?"

I glanced back at Dax, my mouth open for several seconds before I looked over at her. "We're still trying to figure that out. I guess it will be a surprise for all of us."

Penny nodded and slipped the check onto the table between us. She looked at the both of us and grinned, some private thought not quite visible on her face. "Okay, let me know if you need anything else, and have fun. I'll see you tomorrow."

My nerves spurred into action again, and I tried to avoid eye contact for several seconds after, even though I knew Dax was studying me.

"If you could dress up as anything, what would you be?" he asked.

I snapped my eyes to him, the sincerity on his face causing me to think.

My mind scrolled through the things I'd wanted to be for past Halloweens. Only a handful of my costumes were actually something I wanted to wear. My mom had gone through a phase where she wanted to dress Zane and me in identical or matching outfits, meaning neither of us got to choose.

"I mean, I wanted to be a unicorn when I was five," I said, grinning.

Dax grimaced and nodded. He waved his hands. "If that's

what you want to do, then I'm sure we can rig the lights to make it look like that."

I laughed, slapping the table once. "No, I wouldn't do that to you. I hadn't thought of making something fun out of the lights. I've always enjoyed art, so maybe something that showed that?"

Dax chuckled, sitting back. He had his head tilted somewhat as he stared at me, that adorable grin on his face. "Okay, I'm liking this idea much better than rainbows and horns, but it's still kind of broad. What can we do to dress up like art?" He tapped his lips several times, his gaze bouncing around the restaurant while I couldn't take my eyes from him.

An idea hit me, sending a charge of excitement through my body. I loved that he wanted to make things interesting. "What if we put some lights on a painting pallet? Then we could dress you up as the canvas with lights going around the outside of it to highlight."

"Please tell me you're not going to turn me into the Mona Lisa?" He stuck out his lower lip, and I burst out laughing.

Why he wanted to cover up this side of him all the time, I wouldn't know. The Dax sitting in front of me was more real than any guy I'd ever known, more relatable too. As I got to know him, I wanted to spend more time with him, and my feelings of attraction spiked.

"What if we buck the famous part and do something a little different?" I asked, stirring the remnants of my shake with my straw.

"Wow, Kate Adams wanting to think outside the box on her own dance theme? I take a girl out for a milkshake to break curfew, and she surprises me." Dax raised his eyebrows like he was a little kid waiting for cake.

Trying to avoid his gaze, I slurped my milkshake through the straw and then gave him a small smile. He finished the last two bites of his brownie sundae and slid the bowl to the middle of the table.

I tried to think of all the options we had for our costumes and how we were going to assemble them before the dance tomorrow. That's when the phone rang, the tone I'd set for my mother blasting through. I pulled it out of my purse and saw the time was 10:01.

I glanced up at Dax, who'd already pulled out a twenty-dollar bill and dropped it on the table. He reached his hand over and helped me from the seat.

"Let's go, Cinderella. I'd rather my car not turn into a pumpkin on the drive to your house."

I smiled wide, surprised by his humor but also trying to ease the knot of tension in my stomach. I was going to be in major trouble, but for some reason, being with Dax lessened the worry quite a bit.

It wasn't like I'd always been like this, just since my mom married my stepdad; I wanted her to be happy. But that was going to have to change and soon. My sanity depended on it.

CHAPTER 17

DAX

I probably should've taken Kate right home after the game. With the way she sat next to me on the way back to her house, stiff and staring out the front window, I hoped she wouldn't be grounded into next week. My father had only grounded me once, way back when I was maybe twelve, after I hit a ball through one of the neighbors' trailer windows. From the way Kate's mom had looked at me earlier that night when I picked her up, like I was prey and she was a large animal, I started to worry for Kate.

She waved goodbye and slipped into the house, the lights all ablaze. I glanced at the clock on the dashboard. 10:06 pm. Not bad. I'd driven through a shortcut I knew and sped as fast as I could to get her home. Hopefully her mother would forgive six minutes.

I made my way home and parked the car, turning it off. Sitting in the silence, I pulled out my phone and opened up a new text message.

I hope you're not in too much trouble.

A few minutes ticked by, and I waited, hoping she'd text

me back. I could've gone inside, but I knew the sound of the message would probably wake up one of my siblings, even though one of the lights was on through the trailer window.

I'll survive.

My breath hitched, and I worried that I'd ruined things with her. Since when had I gone from telling myself I couldn't be with Kate to hoping there would be more time spent together?

My fingers tapped out a few words, but another message came from her.

Thanks for taking me with you tonight. I had a lot of fun. And I owe you for the shake.

I chuckled a moment before the words hit me. Did she mean that because she didn't want me to get the wrong impression that it was somehow a date? Or because I'd said that to her about buying all of Bree's dance clothes?

I thought through it a few minutes, trying to figure out what to text her that wouldn't make things awkward.

You're fine. I owe you a lot more for all those clothes you bought Bree.

When no answer came through, I typed, *Sleep well. I'll see you tomorrow.*

Would she be okay? I knew I was only interpreting what happened over a text message, but I didn't want to do anything that took the smile away from the girl I was falling head over heels for.

It took a lot longer for me to fall asleep that night, and even when I did, I dreamt of Kate being locked in a prison cell because she'd spent time with me. Her mother was the warden, and when I knocked on her door because she didn't pick me up for the dance, I thought her mom was going to either arrest me or shoot me. I might have woken up sweating, the emotions of reality still running high from the nightmare.

I walked into work at seven, before the garage even opened for the day. Doc was already under a car, his long legs spread out below one of the cars that had been there a time or two.

I squatted down, trying to see what he was replacing this time. "Hey, Doc. Where do you want me to start today?"

He used his legs to propel the creeper he was laying on out from under the car so he could see me and grinned. "Dax, you're here early."

"I thought I'd come in and get some stuff done before we open. I, uh, I'm going to a dance today and will need to leave a bit early for the activity." I moved my boot across the floor, feeling more than self-conscious under Doc's eye. He was like a second dad, or third if I counted all the punishments I'd gotten from Mr. McKee. I knew he'd either lecture me or give me a hard time about finally going on a date.

"It's about time you enjoy some of the high school experience," Doc said, leaning forward with a wrench in his hand. "Who are you going with?"

A picture of Kate popped into my mind, and I couldn't help but grin. "Her name is Kate Adams. She's the student body president."

"Adams, Adams," Doc said, mumbling to himself. A few seconds later, he snapped his fingers. "Aw, yes. Her mom's name is Karla, right?"

I shrugged, trying to remember if that was true. "I think so?"

"Good family. I knew Karla and her first husband, David. They were a pretty great pair and lived close to us before they moved to their new house. They were always fun to hang out with and good people. I was sad to hear he'd died in a car accident, but I hadn't kept in touch for a while."

My thoughts turned back to the night before, and curiosity won over. "Was Karla always really controlling?"

Doc studied my face, a hint of a smile around his lips. "She had some moments that were a little controlling, but for the most part, she and David seemed like a good team. Why do you ask?"

"She has Kate's schedule so packed with things to make her look good on college applications that Kate can barely breathe. I know I wouldn't survive doing all that." I picked up a screwdriver from the rolling tool table next to me, turning it over in my hands.

"I think Karla had to work a lot once he was gone. They had a lot of bills, and supporting the family took time. Maybe she's just hoping to help Kate avoid something like that in her life?"

I turned over Doc's words a few times, realizing he was probably right about that. If Kate's mom went through even a fraction of what my family did every month, the wondering if there was going to be money for food or if we could pay for all the activities and fees we had with three kids, I could see why she'd want to push Kate to get a good education.

I set to work, my thoughts turning to Kate often, causing my excitement to mount about the upcoming dance. I shouldn't be this way, should be shutting down my feelings for her, but there was a sliver of hope that she'd return them.

I'll be by your house in about thirty minutes to pick you up.

I glanced at the time and noticed I'd been working for nearly four hours. It had passed as if it were only a few minutes. I loved my job, but work had never gone by that fast for me.

After wiping my hands off on a cloth, I replied, *Sounds good.*

"I'm heading out, Doc. Let me know if you need me to do anything on Monday."

"Enjoy your date. Have some fun for once, Dax. You deserve it." Doc grinned at me from behind the cash register.

I strolled out of the shop, counting down the minutes until I'd see Kate. This was either going to be a night to remember or a date that would cause me the beginnings of heartbreak.

"Why would you ask *him* to the dance?" my mom asked, her face pinched like she'd just eaten a pickle.

I had just taken several bags of supplies out to the shed where Dax and I would design our shirts. I must have left my phone on the counter because it was in her hand, and she kept waving it around like it held a ton of secrets. I was just glad she didn't have the passcode to see all my text messages to him.

"Why not? He's never been to a dance, and he's part of the senior committee." I was trying to stay calm and relaxed, making light of it even though my mother looked like she was ready to explode.

She closed her eyes, pinching the bridge of her nose with her thumb and forefinger. "Katie, there are so many kids you could've invited. Are you trying to date him because he's a baseball player? Is that some sort of trend right now?"

It took everything in me to keep from laughing. A trend to date a certain sport athlete? It was probably something she'd read in one of her articles about trying to relate to teens.

"Mom, it's nothing." I opened the fridge, grabbing the bottle of orange juice. "It's just a dance. You'll still cook dinner, right?"

My mom sighed and nodded. "Of course. I've got all the things for a Halloween dinner party."

I clapped my hands and grinned. "Thank you! It's been so long since we've had our Spooky Dinner. I'm excited to share it with my friends."

I walked out the door, breathing a sigh of relief that I'd dodged a bullet there.

* * *

"Okay, let's figure out how we're going to connect all this stuff, shall we?" I said, glancing up at Dax. His eyes kept moving over the table full of glow sticks.

"Got a little excited about this, did you?" he said, the corner of his mouth inching up as he glanced in my direction, a twinkle in his eye.

I waved over the small packages filled with glow sticks and shook my head. "Of course not. This is for sure an appropriate amount of glow sticks for a dance. Have you never been to a black-light party?"

"No," he said, chuckling. "Have you?"

"Well, no. But this will be good for us. We have plenty of options for how we want it to look. And I even have some glow-in-the-dark paint to use on the shirts."

He was right. It was a bit of overkill, but I'd bought everything that morning and hadn't wanted to miss anything since I wouldn't have the chance to run back to the store. I'd already experienced the "I forgot something" twelve times on the day of a dance and never had time to finish my costume before it was time to leave.

I'd had to guess on his size when it came to the black shirt, and after seeing him climb the walls at the rock-climbing activity, I wondered if I should've gotten one a little smaller so I could just stare at his arms all night. Or not. Because I didn't need that kind of thing distracting me from my goals. If only my brain would really be convinced of that.

Dax leaned on the table, his eyebrow raised as he asked, "Did you get in trouble for being late last night?"

I blew out a breath and rolled my eyes. "At first. But then I just said something about helping out with some ideas about the dance, and she was okay with it. At least she wasn't physically at the game, or I wouldn't have been able to claim that." We both laughed at that.

After a second, I said, "My turn for a question. Are you really the bad boy everyone thinks you are?"

His eyes locked onto mine, and I was sure all the breath had been squeezed out of my body. "What do you think?"

I shook my head and smiled. "I don't buy it. The guy who works long hours at a garage, plays baseball, and pays for his sister's dance? Yeah, you're the unsung hero."

Dax's cheeks flushed, and I grinned. When he didn't say anything, I continued, surprised by my own words. "How many people have you kissed?"

His eyes widened, and he said, "What does that have to do with anything?"

"Rumor says you're a playboy. Again, I'm calling it."

"Three."

I didn't think he could get any more red as the color rose up his neck and throughout his cheeks and nose. I was kind of shocked at that number, and for some reason, my defenses rose, like I felt left out that I wasn't part of that number.

"Well, what kind of design should we do?" Dax asked,

changing the subject quickly. He pressed his palm on the table so his body was inches from mine.

My breathing sped up, and I managed to avoid looking to my right, knowing I'd probably do something to ruin the moment.

"Should we do some kind of baseball thing? That could be fun." I stared at the black shirts, wondering how to paint them to make them look like Dax's favorite sport.

Dax was shaking his head, looking at me like I'd lost my mind. "Do you hear yourself? I like more stuff than just baseball. What I'm asking is, what do you want to go as? I've seen your talents with a paintbrush, and I'm sure you can create just about anything. The question is, what does Kate Adams want to look like tonight?"

I took a deep breath, surprised by the serious tone. I'd never really had anyone ask me what I wanted, instead usually doing everything I could to make it about them, hoping to make them feel good.

Biting my inner lip, I turned to him. "It's almost Halloween. What if we do something with that?"

"Is that what you want to do?" Dax asked, his eyebrow raised.

I let my mind open to the creativity that, for some reason, I locked up more often than I should have. I scrolled through a mental lineup of Halloween ideas—witches, ghosts, skeletons—but none of them seemed like something I wanted to tackle.

A quick glance at the clock showed we had about ninety minutes until we had to be ready for dinner. Luckily, we were out in my stepdad's garage—or man cave, as he liked to call it—so we wouldn't be in the way of my mom and her friend preparing the food for our Spooky Dinner before the dance.

Resting a hand on my hip, I tipped my head back to look

at him. "What if we do some kind of superhero? We can paint on the shirt and then accent it with the glow sticks."

"That sounds pretty awesome, but I'd be willing to dress up as a unicorn if that's what you wanted." His smirk opened the cage of butterflies in my stomach. "But only because it's you." Something about his words was more tender, more real than the joking from before.

A few seconds passed, and I broke my gaze away from him. "Superheroes it is. Who is your favorite superhero?"

"Captain America." Dax did a slow head bob, his lips scrunched, trying to look more intense than he actually was.

"What? Not Thor or Superman?" I asked, opening a bottle of glow-in-the-dark paint.

Dax's hand touched the back of mine, and I paused, a quick bolt of electricity passing between us. "I know I don't look like I'm into comics or anything, but we have to get one thing straight. Captain America and Thor are from Marvel Comics. Superman is from DC Comics."

"Okay," I said, letting my voice trail off. I smiled wider as I saw how adamant he was about teaching me this one thing. Kind of how he was when he explained math.

"Two different universes. But Superman would be my choice from DC." He laughed, the sound hearty and filling. "What about you? Who are you going to be?"

I tapped the dry sponge paintbrush against my lips, trying to remember some of them. "I could be Wonder Woman. Or there are some others, but I can't think of them right now."

Dax leaned back, holding up his hand. "Black Widow, The Wasp. Yeah, I can't remember either." We both laughed at that.

"I think I'll stick with Wonder Woman. Do you want to pull up a picture of the logos on your phone? That will help us with designing the shirt."

As he scrolled through his phone, punching in things, he said, "When you say us, you really mean you, right?"

"What's that supposed to mean?" I asked, glancing his way as I squeezed a small dot of paint onto a paper plate. Not the tools I used for the more delicate art pieces I worked with, but then again, not having to clean the paint board and brushes was going to be nice. I'd just have to be really precise with the brushes I was using.

"Believe me, if you want people to even remotely recognize the character I am, you'll paint mine too." He set his phone down on the table, and a Wonder Woman logo stared at me from the screen.

I leaned in closer to him, raising my pointer finger and waving it back and forth at him. "I don't care if they can recognize it or not. That's the fun of this," I said, waving my hand over the materials on the table. The light in there wasn't the best, even during the later afternoon, and shadows passed over Dax's face.

"I'm not joking when I say I'm not good at anything creative. Machines, math, baseball…that about covers my abilities."

I stared at him and realized the emotions playing on his face were supposed to cover the nerves I could see every once in a while.

I leaned forward, resting my hand on his upper arm, trying to focus on the words I was supposed to use to encourage him instead of the strong muscle beneath my hand.

"Dax, really. Just try it. I'm not making you dress up like a unicorn, but I am making you paint your own shirt."

His expression fell, and he picked up a brush. He slowly dipped it into the paint and froze as he stared at the shirt again.

Fear of failure. I definitely knew that look from all the

times I froze over things. Like math, and an important test. Or having to meet the world at one of my mom's parties.

Taking a step behind him, I placed my hand on his wrist, the touch pulling him out of the trance. "How about I help you at the beginning?"

The piercing gaze of his dark-brown irises caused me to swallow hard for a moment as the tension built between us. For a moment, I thought maybe he was the one who'd kissed me last spring. But after all the time we'd spent together, he would have said something about it, right? The ego he showed the rest of the world would have spilled the beans. For some reason, it didn't quite fit him, and I shook it off.

He nodded and glanced back at the shirt.

Oh boy, what had I been thinking to ask him to the dance? There were too many emotions swirling through me right now. If I wasn't careful, I'd end up wishing I'd never given him the chance in the first place.

CHAPTER 19

DAX

Seeing the determination in Kate's eyes to have me paint my own t-shirt, plus the added pressure of her soft fingers around my wrist, caused my heart to beat rapidly against my rib cage. I'd never had these emotions running through me before, and the light pink of her lips kept drawing my eyes down, wanting to repeat what happened last spring.

"Okay, so Captain America will be an easy one to design. Do you want to start with the star or the circles?" Kate asked, her head peering around my arm. I often forgot how short she was because her personality made her seem inches taller.

"Star sounds like a good idea." My mouth was dry, and the words were barely intelligible.

I glanced around the room, taking in the half-wood-shop/half-television-and-gaming area of the small shed. When she'd said we were coming back to design our outfits after we'd gone rock climbing that morning, I thought more people from the group would have joined us. As much as I liked this alone time with her, the more I was around her, the more attached I felt. How was I going to tame my feelings for her after this dance?

She nodded, moving my arm for me to start the star. "Okay, the easiest thing for me is to start with an outline of the shape I want. Is this the color you want for the star?" She bent my arm for me, accidentally jabbing the brush with the paint against my face, leaving a smear of blue paint across my cheek. It was cold, and I gasped.

Kate dropped my hand and placed both palms over her face, her eyes wide.

"I'm so, so sorry. I really didn't think I was moving your arm that hard, and then it was just, like, whoa," she said, moving her arms to imitate what had happened. She turned to search for something, grabbing a small paper towel at the end of the table.

While she looked that way, I dipped my brush into the paint again and swiped it across her cheek when she turned back.

Her eyes went even wider than before, and her smile revealed her shock.

"I can't believe you just did that," she said, swiping her finger over the wet paint.

I grinned, stretching the brush forward and swiping across her nose. "I was just helping us match."

She giggled, the sound like little bells, and I joined in, feeling more comfortable than I had since my mother died. In a quick movement, she darted around me, and before I could grab her arm, she swiped a section of red from my eye to my jaw.

We moved back and forth, each one adding another brush stroke to the face, until I wrapped my arm around her waist, lifting her and setting her down behind me, allowing me full access to the paint and blocking her away.

"That's not fair," she said, her hand pushing against my middle with surprising force.

I dabbed some yellow just under her eyes, getting transfixed in the sight.

She stole the brush from my hand and swiped it along my chin. Her eyes stilled on mine, her finger resting in the wet paint on my chin. "This is a canvas I think I can work with." Her voice came out breathless and soft, her expression tender and kind.

The pull between us was thick, like cords latching us together. I kept glancing down to her lips, already feeling the nerves in my own sparking, remembering how it happened the last time we kissed.

We leaned in, and I dipped my head a second, watching as she closed her eyes, her long lashes visible. I was about to kiss her, when the knob of the door turned. It didn't take long for me to jump back, knowing I'd be putting up with her mother if she caught us out there kissing.

"Have you two finished yet?" her brother asked, looking less than enthused to be out there. He took a look at both of us and laughed. "Looks like you got more on your faces than on the shirts."

Kate huffed and waved him away with her hand. "We'll be done in a few minutes. Just go out."

I saw the redness of her cheeks and wondered if she was embarrassed that we'd almost kissed or that we almost got caught.

Instead of walking out the door, Zane plopped down in a chair by the door and shook his head. "Mom said I'm supposed to stay here until you finish. Something about needing a chaperone or something," he said, mumbling the last part. "Hurry up, though. I was right in the middle of my game when she made me come out here."

Nothing like having the mom be suspicious about us out

here by ourselves. Then again, I could understand that. Karsten and Bree were my siblings, but if they were in a similar situation, I'd have sicced a watchdog on them too.

Kate flashed me a guilty smile, ducking her head as she rolled her lips in and picked up the paintbrush from the ground. "Okay, well. How about we race to see who finishes first?" She raised her eyebrows, heightening the challenge.

I tried to hold back a grin when I said, "What does the winner get?"

Her eyes flashed, and we both looked over at her brother for a few seconds. His eyes were engrossed in something on his phone. "Let's leave it up to the winner."

Challenge accepted.

CHAPTER 20

KATE

I did not win the competition. Dax spread paint around like a five-year-old, and I did everything I could to breathe in through my nose and out through my mouth at the sight. I wasn't usually a control freak, but that all changed when I was dealing with paints and brushes.

When I asked Dax what the reward was, he said, "You'll see."

That response sent both a shiver and a thrill running through me. Zane was just glad he could go back inside and finish his game.

We changed once inside and helped each other with the other glow sticks, adding them all over to our ensemble. By the time we finished, it was time for the group to arrive for dinner. But it was difficult to do anything but look at Dax and remember his face as he leaned in, the tension between us so thick that even my mother's supersharp knife set wouldn't be able to cut through it.

"You guys look, um, awesome," Brynn said once inside the door. She gave me that look like, "Are you really sure that's what you want to wear?" and then continued into the kitchen with her date trailing behind her. Penny and Jake and then Nate and Colt and their dates all came in a few minutes later, and we started the meal.

"Okay, wow. I didn't realize we'd have half of the baseball team here," my mother said between clenched teeth, meaning she was trying to be supportive but I would definitely hear about it later.

She grabbed a couple of platters from the island in the kitchen and brought them over to the dining table, spreading them out along the table. "One of our favorite things when Kate was growing up was to do a spooky dinner. So here are a bunch of edible options," she said, emphasizing the edible, "that will help bring the spirit of the holiday."

"Thank you, ma'am," Dax said quietly but loud enough for her to hear.

She turned to him and paused, her face without emotion until she finally nodded and said, "You're welcome." The tone wasn't really warm, but neither was it cold. That was the most indecisive my mother had ever been about anything in my life.

We chatted while we ate, reminiscing about the rock climbing from the morning and the boys swapping some stories about a baseball game last spring. I hadn't seen Dax smile that wide in a long time. It seemed like he was having fun.

"Okay, everyone. We should probably get going," I said, checking the large clock on the far wall. The junior committee was in charge of the dance, but I always worried that they'd still be setting up the decorations when people were coming into the gym for the dance.

"Are you sure you don't want to make a dramatic entrance?" Nate joked.

There were times I wished I could smack the guy, but when he wasn't trying to be so cool, he was somewhat chill.

"We can help them get things ready, right?" Dax glanced around the table, looking at all the guys, the tone of his voice more serious than I'd heard him speak around them. The shift in the room caused me to smile as it was usually Jake's words that they all listened to.

Everyone stood, helping clear the table and heading out the door. We piled into a couple of cars and headed over to the school.

I drove my crossover vehicle with Brynn and her date, Garrett, sitting in the back of the car whispering about something. I glanced over at Dax and tried to figure out how to say what I wanted to.

"Thanks, for back there." I pointed my finger toward the house and turned my gaze behind me so I could reverse out of the driveway. When I put it into drive, I noticed the confusion on Dax's face.

"What do you mean?" he asked.

"I mean for standing up for me when it came to the whole getting-there-early thing. My friends give me a hard time."

"That's something, considering Penny is scared to death of being late to anything." Dax chuckled, and I gave him a small smile, realizing how right he was.

I sighed, nodding. "I know, but I don't have to put up with a lecture from my mother if I show up early."

The rest of the drive was relatively quiet, chatting here and there about a few things, but mostly my stomach was wrapped up in nerves. I couldn't get the smell of him from earlier in the man cave out of my senses, and the thought of him kissing me was something I wanted more than I'd thought up until now. I was getting in deep and too fast.

It took some time to check on everything, but Dax finally pulled me onto the dance floor, surprising me by the way he led the dances, making it more fun than just swaying back and forth. At least he wasn't stepping on my toes like some of my past dance dates.

"Where did you learn how to dance like this?" I asked, tilting my head back to glance up at him.

His smile was sad, his eyes looking far away and glazed. "My mom." He turned his attention back to me and smiled a bit wider. "She would give me dance lessons while we cleaned up from dinner. It's one of the things I'll never forget about her."

All the warm fuzzies took over my chest, and I could imagine a slightly younger version of Dax, probably towering over his mother like he did me, listening to her as she instructed him on what to do.

"Those are the memories to be cherished, for sure." I dropped my gaze, focusing on the blobs of paint on Dax's chest. Memories of my own father crept up, the simple fun times we always had when he was done with work. He'd been a carpenter, usually working long hours to help support the family. But when he was home, he was present. One of the gifts I would be grateful for in the years to come.

We danced through several songs, and I was on cloud nine. The way he held my hand as we danced and then how he placed his hand on the small of my back when we left to get a drink or move through a crowd had my stomach doing some serious gymnastics.

Once it was close to the end, we headed back to my house once more to watch a movie in the theater room with everyone but Brynn and Garrett, who had to go home early.

Several minutes into the movie, I heard my mother whisper a few feet away. Her tight expression was illuminated by the light cast from the screen. I stood, feeling the loss of excitement I'd had from sitting next to Dax during a movie, and scooted out of the row and through the door where my mother waited in the light. I could tell from the stiffness in her back as I followed her out into the hall that she wasn't happy.

"What do you need, Mom?" I asked in a harsh whisper.

"Why didn't you tell me you were planning to come back here after the dance?" She was waving her hands, a sign that she was even madder about something than I realized.

I frowned, taking a step back and folding my arms across my chest. "Since when do you have a problem with me bringing people here? You're always complaining that we hang out at everyone else's house, and now you don't want us here?"

Her jaw twitched back and forth, the muscle pulsing a time or two. She shifted her weight to another leg and said, "What happened to all the people you hung out with on Senior Committee?"

"What do you mean?" I asked, my lungs squeezing as I knew where she was going with this. Instead of responding, I waited, wanting her to say what she felt for once.

"I mean, I know Penny is dating Jake and all, but did you all have to start taking on with the baseball kids? They aren't the best influence in your life."

Frustration surged in my throat, and my cheeks heated, knowing I was going to be replaying this moment for days after this.

"Mom, they're good kids. They're not as crazy as you make them sound, and I really like hanging out with them, especially Dax." I bit down on the side of my lip, wishing I could go back and unsay those last two words. It would tip her off like a rabid dog.

"I get that, Kate. But you have a future. You have so many possibilities, so much potential for a great life. Don't waste it like I did."

"Are you saying you regret your time with Dad?" My tone bit, and from the shocked look on her face, it bit hard.

She shook her head and reached out to me, rubbing her hands up and down my upper arms. "No, of course not. I'm just saying there are things I wish I would have done. Finishing my degree would have been one of them. So that when things happened, I wouldn't have had to scrape to get us by. Preparation is the key, just like I always say."

"Okay, Mom. What are you saying?"

"I'd prefer you don't get attached, not yet anyway. Just have fun. Enjoy your last year and leave the relationships to the future."

Tears surged to my eyes, and I turned, walking back into the theater room without giving her a response. I suddenly wished I could just go upstairs and cuddle up in my blankets instead of playing hostess, but I would just have to grin and bear it, like I did with so many other things in my life.

When I sat next to Dax again, I curled up closer this time, grateful when he draped his arm over me. Too many emotions were pumping through me, trying to win out, and I was just too tired to care right now. I'd figure things out in the morning, but for now, I enjoyed the comfort I felt sitting right next to Dax.

CHAPTER 21

DAX

I wasn't sure what had changed when Kate left the room for a few minutes and then came back, but I wasn't going to say no to her snuggled next to me. I'd wanted to follow her out and help with whatever, but when I saw her mother there next to us, I knew it was a conversation best left to them. But I could tell something was bothering her when she returned, as her laughter always came a half-second later than everyone else's.

The movie was loud and long, and Kate falling asleep against me was the best feeling in the world. I loved the smell of her, the way she looked so peaceful like she wasn't trying to please the whole world at the same time.

When the movie finally ended and someone turned on the lights, Kate only shifted, staying asleep next to me. I didn't want to wake her up, but I needed to get a ride home at some point. I could always go with Penny and Jake and crash at his house for the night. With his dad moved out, he was more willing to have me over than before, something I could relate to. Well, the knowing why he hadn't wanted anyone over before.

"Hey, Sleeping Beauty," I said, shifting my shoulder up and down to try and wake her.

She blinked a couple of times, her eyes small slits against the bright lights above. "Is the movie over?" she asked, sitting up and staring at me as much as she could while blinking.

I nodded. "News flash: they got together."

We'd watched some romantic comedy that all the girls agreed we should watch, and I'd actually kind of enjoyed it. I hadn't had time to watch a movie in longer than I could remember, usually running from one thing to another.

The thing that surprised me most was that I hadn't fallen asleep as well, but it must have been the excitement to be there with Kate that kept me watching the show, not the fact that the movie had been about some mystery crush and how they'd handled that situation. It only made me want to keep our first kiss a secret even longer.

She smiled, rubbing her eyes with her fists, and then stood, reaching her arms high into the air to stretch. "It's one of my favorites."

"What is it that you like about it?" I ventured to ask. There were several things that intrigued me, and I wondered if that was really how girls thought about love and relationships.

"I guess it's the fact that her best friend was the guy she fell in love with. It's just so cute how she doesn't realize it until the very end."

I pinched my lips together. Was she saying she could only like a guy if he was her best friend first? "What about the mystery? He'd been writing her notes for a long time, and she didn't even try to investigate who was sending them to her." I was getting dangerously close to spilling the secret at this point, and I needed to be careful.

Her mouth opened and closed, but nothing escaped. This

was the first time I'd ever seen her flustered, and I wondered what she would say.

"Maybe she just liked that it was a mystery, something to get excited about. But if she found out who the person behind the letters was, it would ruin the magic." She kept her gaze a couple inches to the right of me, and a stab of sadness pierced my chest. I'd hoped she would remember the kiss from last spring. But Nate's phrase about her friends telling her to get over the Masked Kisser came to mind. Had she actually done it and moved on? So was she hanging out with me because she wanted to or to irritate her mother?

I could just move on, make sure I graduated, and figure out the rest of my life. I didn't have time for waffling.

Kate grabbed her keys from a bowl in the entryway, following the rest of the group out the door.

"Kate, you don't have to take me home. I can go with one of the others."

She frowned, her lips puckered and eyebrows drawn together. "Why? I asked you to the dance. I can drop you off."

The way she said it, I wondered if I'd been misinterpreting her tone for the past couple of weeks. But then again, it had been a long night. It was possible she was just tired and things would be normal again on Monday. I hoped she'd be back to her normal self on Monday.

CHAPTER 22

KATE

I spent most of Sunday in my room, cleaning, organizing, or just lying on the bed and staring up at the ceiling. I didn't come out for much more than to grab a snack and head back up, not in the mood to talk to others in my family. Then the next few days sped past, and I kept wondering if I was going to make it to the next weekend at the rate I was going.

The conflicting emotions inside me warred against the need to please my mother and all the other people in my life. I really liked Dax, though I wasn't sure if he liked me more than to spend time with me at a dance and then the mandatory time during Senior Committee. But the fact that she'd basically implied I needed to stay away from him made me both angry and frustrated.

I waved hello to Dax in the halls and talked a bit, feeling that same chemistry again in fourth period, but once we left that room, it was like the spell had broken and panic settled in, making it so I didn't know what to do.

It would be so easy to just say, "Forget my mom," and move on, do what I wanted to do. But there were so many things she'd gone through while married to my father and then after he passed away. All that experience had to count for something.

"Hey, you want to come to the baseball game tonight?" Penny asked, shutting her locker after school let out Thursday afternoon.

"They have a game?" I asked, trying to remember if I'd talked to Dax about that.

"Yeah, it's just down the road at Groveton Park. They play tonight and then again Friday and Saturday." She paused, her small smile alerting me that she was waiting for my response.

I had to teach the dance class and pick up Bree on the way. It would be fun to see Dax in action, if only to support as a friend.

A friend that would love to kiss him.

There were several moments when I'd replayed the scene in my stepdad's man cave, my breath hitching and the air almost crackling as he leaned in. If only Zane hadn't barged in, I would have known what it felt like to kiss Dax.

"Yeah, I'll meet you there. I have cheer right now, and then I can make it after. What time does the game start?" I twirled a piece of hair around my finger. It usually helped me clear my head and figure out what I needed to do with situations in my life.

"Seven."

"Sounds good. I'll meet you there."

I strolled out to my car, turned it on, and pulled out of the parking lot. Again, I thought about the near kiss, which in turn, brought up the Masked Kisser from months ago. Some of the details were fuzzy, but I didn't think I could forget his lips on mine.

As I pulled up to the Stratton trailer, I saw Dax's car sitting outside, and my heart rate sped up, excitement flowing through me. I got out and knocked on the front door.

Dax opened it, a small smile on his face. He turned and called over his shoulder, "Bree! Kate is here." When he looked my way, he said, "How was your day?"

The way he said it, with that genuine sincerity, set my insides on fire. "I'm good. Just another day." I paused for a minute and then said, "You have a game tonight, huh?"

I pointed to his jersey, which he hadn't yet tucked into his pants.

He looked down and pulled it out a bit near the chest before glancing back up. "Uh, yeah. We play Groveton tonight. You should come if you have time after Bree's class." The hope on his face was evident.

I smiled. "I'll try to make it." I didn't have much going on after class for once, and I was grateful for that. As much as I didn't want to ruin things with him, I was still curious about his life. He always made me feel like the best person in the world.

"It would be fun to have you there." He flexed his arms a bit, his lips puckered in exaggeration. "I'll have to try and hit a home run or two while you're there."

"Really?" I said dryly.

He shook his head with a laugh. "I'm just kidding. I've hit a couple of home runs, but I'm usually a gap hitter. Whatever gets me on base, I'll take it."

I liked the honesty there, grateful that the arrogant façade hadn't stuck around for long.

Bree came to the door, and as we walked back to the car, she practically bounced until she got into her seat, chatting about everything that happened during the day.

I glanced up and saw Dax staring in my direction. I smiled at him, knowing I was in more trouble with my heart than I should be.

Cheer class went by faster than usual, and it helped that all the dancers were actually listening instead of playing around and doing whatever they wanted. I dropped Bree back off and headed home to change my clothes and do my best to look casual but good.

When I drove to Groveton Park, I wondered what in the world I was doing there. It had been a long time since I'd gone to something at that complex, but the fact that I knew the guys playing made it more fun to attend—and my crush for the catcher was both exciting and scary.

I kept replaying my mother's words in my head, about how she wished she'd been more prepared for life without my dad. But people went to college and had relationships at the same time. Why couldn't I do that?

Then again, did Dax even think of me like that?

I found Penny and Serena sitting in the stands on the top bench, and they each slid over, opening up a spot for me in the packed stands.

"Wow, I didn't realize this many people would be here." I glanced out at the field, staring at the back of the catcher and trying to hold back a grin.

"We're playing Groveton," Serena said, laughing. "Our cross-town rivals are sure to bring a big crowd."

I shrugged. "True. I hadn't really thought of that." I hadn't thought much through clearly over the past week, and I wished I could figure out what I should do about Dax. Then there was still the possibility of finding the Masked Kisser, which had a renewed hope filling me.

We cheered and laughed, making the evening one of the best moments I'd had in a long time, aside from my time with Dax. I hadn't had any extra activities forced on me by my mother, and being free like this was something I needed to do more often.

After the game ended, the three of us waited outside the

dugout for the guys to appear. Penny ran up and hugged Jake, the two of them talking about the plays, using words that flew right over my head. That's what you get when a softball player dates a shortstop.

Serena and I just glanced at each other and laughed, not understanding a word of it.

She walked up to Ben a little more casually, and they shared a quick kiss before she wrapped her arms around his middle, looking a lot like I would with Dax if I were to go up and hug him.

I felt the pressure as Dax finally came around the dugout, focused on shifting things around in his bag as his equipment stuck out in all directions. I glanced in the direction of my friends to see them engrossed in their significant others, and I knew I had to do something. But instead, I pulled out my phone, scrolling mindlessly through my Quickstagram account as I watched every movement out of my periphery.

When he finally stood, opening his water bottle, his gaze bouncing around the small crowd, I was pretty sure I stopped breathing. Sure, I couldn't see the sparkle in his eyes when he looked at me from this distance, but I liked him a whole lot more than I should have.

Then those feelings were overshadowed by the way my mom had described getting through life unprepared, and I suddenly wanted to run to give myself more time to sort through my feelings.

"Hey," Dax said, strolling up to me while he took a swig from his water bottle. "I'm so glad you came."

I glanced up and smiled, pretending I hadn't noticed every move he'd made since he came into sight.

"Good game. It was fun to see you all play." I gestured over to the other two couples and bounced on the balls of my feet a couple of times. "You had some great hits."

He shrugged. "Not really great, but they did the job." His

eyes stared through me, and he tucked his right hand into the back pocket of his baseball pants, looking more relaxed than I'd seen him in a while.

From his level of play on the field, he was really good and able to handle just about everything Ben threw at him, especially all the balls in the dirt that game. Serena had been shaking her head throughout the whole game, mumbling something about having to get Ben out of his head after the game. I guess perfection was still a hurdle for them sometimes, but Serena did a good job of helping him through it.

"Do you have another game tonight?" I asked, trying to find something else to say. Why was it that when he first walked into Ms. Shiels's room after getting into that fight, I was able to talk to him, even flirt a little, like I didn't have a care in the world? And now I liked him, and it seemed as though my tongue was still numb from the stuff the dentist uses to do cavities.

He nodded. "Yeah, we have one of the night games. It's always kind of fun to play under the lights. Almost like we're in the big leagues."

I grinned and nodded, understanding that a bit. Dancing in the bright lights on stage used to bring me the same kind of thrill. "I wish I could stay. But I want to hear all about how the next game goes." I pointed a finger at him, trying to ensure he got my meaning. I was already dancing in some hot water when it came to all this, but the pull I felt toward Dax tended to cloud my rational judgment sometimes.

"I'll let you know. If it's too late tonight, I'll see you in class tomorrow."

He took a step forward, reaching his hands around me and holding on to me for several moments. The mixture of his cologne with sweat and dirt made me smile. It wasn't like I'd ever dated someone who was semi-athletic, and something about this drew me to him even more.

"We're going to head out," Penny said, tapping my shoulder when Dax pulled away.

I nodded in her direction and then turned my gaze to Dax's face again. "I'll let you get back to games, but I can't wait to hear more about this." I reached up and wrapped my arms around his neck, pulling him down a bit closer to my height. I kissed his cheek softly, the light stubble there tickling my lips.

"Thanks again for coming. I'll see you later." He stood back and waved a bit as I walked away, stealing a glance again here and there.

As I strolled next to the girls over to the parking lot, I knew I was getting worse and worse at all this.

"What's up, Kate?" Serena asked, waving her hand in front of my face.

"Just sorting through some things." I wasn't trying to be vague, but there was only so much space in my brain at the moment.

"I've been there." She took a few longer strides and then rounded on me, causing me to make an abrupt halt. "But what's going on with you and Dax?"

That was the one thing I really didn't want to talk about tonight, because I didn't really have an answer for that anyway. "Who knows? I mean, I like him, but my mom is already breathing down my neck from the dance last week. She doesn't like the idea of me being in a relationship and even brought up the time before she married my stepdad."

"What happened before that?" Serena asked. We'd met after my mom married my stepdad, and I'd never really told anyone about it but Penny.

"When Kate's dad died, her mom had to take on a few jobs at a time to pay the bills, until she met Kate's stepdad. So it's kind of the reason why Karla is a little intense when it comes to life goals." Penny gave a grim smile and kicked at a pebble in the way as we walked along the sidewalk, finally making it to the parking lot from the field.

Serena pursed her lips, and I just waited for the sarcasm that would erupt from her. "Says the girl with life goals the size of Mt. Vesuvius."

We all laughed at that, and I loved the fact that my friends could be real about things.

"She's very intense, but I know she means well." I twirled a piece of hair that had fallen out of my ponytail, going through all the emotions I'd felt in the past ten minutes.

"Kate, come on," Serena said, tapping my arm. "She's over-the-top intense. And you follow along a lot more than you let on."

I took that back about loving my friends being real. This was something I wasn't ready to deal with just yet. My voice sounded strangled when I spoke again. "I was there during those times when she'd come home bone-tired from wait-ressing, and then as a cashier for the gas station. It's why she went back to school to become a school counselor right after she married Bill." With Bill's business, she'd never had to work, but she didn't want to be put in the same situation again if something happened to my stepdad.

I took several breaths, realizing my voice had grown in intensity and my chest was heaving with the frustration.

Penny touched my elbow. "Girl, you're fine. It'll be okay. We're just saying you deserve a little more room for things, some more free time to figure out who you are and what you want to be when you grow up." Her warm smile caused the rest of the anger to fizzle, and I nodded.

"So, has Dax taken over Masked Kisser?" Serena asked, wiggling her eyebrows at me.

I sighed. She was like a bear after lunch. "I don't know. I mean, I really like Dax. But what if I keep looking for MK and he doesn't end up being as great as Dax? Or what if I start dating Dax and my mother freaks out?"

"What's she going to do?" Penny asked, surprising me with the ferocity in her tone. "The worst she can do is ground you, but the benefit to that is you won't be worn out trying to serve every person in this city before you head off to college."

She was right, and I hated to admit it. I'd done so much in the last two years that everything just made me tired to even think about. All I wanted to do was sit down and paint. And somehow get a scholarship so I wouldn't have to mooch off my stepdad.

"I better get home, you guys. I've still got to read for English tomorrow. See you!"

As I drove out of the parking lot in my car, tears slid down my cheeks. How was I going to survive until college? It wasn't forever away, but there were days when I wished it would just rush by so I could have the real kind of freedom I craved.

CHAPTER 23

DAX

Of course, after Kate left I finally hit a home run. We'd barely won the game she'd come to and I'd only hit little singles rolling into the outfield, but at least those hits had scored runs. This pitch came in, and it was in the sweet spot. With a quick swing, I connected the bat with the ball, the ping and feeling of the contact adding to my adrenaline.

I glanced up into the stands, hoping she was there for just a little bit longer to see it. She'd been nervous after the first game, but it was better than the lukewarm feeling I'd gotten from her after the dance and throughout the two fourth-period classes we'd had together since then.

We ended up losing the game despite my three-run dinger, and I was irritated that we'd have to play extra games throughout the rest of the weekend to have a hope of making it to the tournament finals. The other guys were so worried about college coaches, but as much as I loved baseball, I wasn't sure I would make it playing in college.

I was just trying to find an escape from the mundane of school and work, both of which weren't awful, but I needed the variety and the rush of throwing out the best player on the other team as he tried to steal second base.

The thought of college had crossed my mind a time or two, but then my dad's words about being happy with where we already were spread over my mind. Was I the kind of guy who just gave up and let life happen to him? Or was I willing to go seize what I wanted and move on from there?

Our coach gave us the typical after-game speech about needing to cut down on the errors and execute the play calls when we had runners on base, most of which I had already committed to memory from all the past games we'd had with this team.

I untied my cleats, feeling the strain in my upper thighs from squatting down for so long today. Catching was something I had to work into, and it had been a few months since I'd played two three-hour games almost back-to-back.

"How are things going with you and Kate?" Nate asked, turning his cleats over and dumping out a bunch of sand. He'd dived for a ball on the line during the last inning and had made a sweet grab to keep the runner on third base. Too bad Cleaver, our second starting pitcher, had given up a home run on the next pitch anyway.

I shrugged, picking at the grass around us instead of looking up at him. "Nothing is going on between us."

"But you want there to be, right?" Colt asked, pulling off his socks next to me. I shifted over, trying to avoid the breeze sending the smell of rank feet in my direction.

"I don't know, guys. I mean, I have to focus on school and actually graduating. My grandmother would flip if I don't graduate. And I want to be there, holding up the state championship trophy next spring. I can't be with her in a relationship."

Jake shook his head. "Please, man. Look at Penny and me. Sometimes a relationship makes it so you have someone to lean on all the time, someone to build you up when you strike out three times in a row." His face went sour, probably replaying those at-bats in the last game.

As much as I wanted to argue with them that having people in my life sometimes made things even more lonely, the idea of it warmed something in my chest.

"I think you need to tell her you were her secret kiss last spring," Ben said, sitting down next to us. He'd already finished packing up his bags and changed into shoes. It was late, but sitting there, not having somewhere to dart off to, made the time with the guys a little repose, something I needed to get recharged.

"What good will that do me? 'Hey, Kate, I'm the awkward guy that kissed you last spring. Will you be my girlfriend?' No! Girls don't do that." Anger surged, but it wasn't directed at my friends and teammates. It was directed at myself. Because as much as I wanted a relationship with her, I was freaked out of my mind at the fact that as easily as she could say she liked me, she could also reject me.

Jake bent his legs and draped his arms around them, his stare causing me to turn away. "Dax, it's all about the leap. You're just going to have to figure out how to tell her and see where things go. If Kate isn't the one who will like you in return, then you'll just keep working, keep moving on, and you'll eventually find someone else."

As much as I wanted that to be the case, telling her about the kiss was something I worried about more than even college coaches sitting in the stands.

"I'll figure it out," I finally said.

We sat there a few more minutes, talking about different things, but my mind was somewhere else, swirling with what I'd have to do and soon. I didn't want to lead myself along if I didn't have a chance with Kate. And I was already teetering on that edge.

CHAPTER 24

KATE

When I arrived home after the game, I could feel something strange in the air, and it didn't take too long to realize what it was. I walked into the kitchen, setting my purse on the counter as I removed the jacket I'd worn to the game.

"Where have you been?" my mother asked as she walked out of her bedroom. I could see a smidge of frustration on her face, as well as triumph, like she'd won a game.

"I went to the baseball game with Penny and Serena." I strode over to the cabinet and pulled out a glass. Without glancing at her, I stuck the glass into the dispenser in the fridge.

"I don't know why you continue to hang out with those two. Brynn is almost just as bad too." She didn't sound happy about it, but I'd grown so used to this argument, and as much as I wanted to please her in most things, giving up my group of friends was the one option I wouldn't give up.

"They're good girls, Mom." I took a sip of my water, turning to face her as I did so.

She sighed, her way of saying she would concede on that alone.

"Just don't keep missing your activities. I don't need another call from the shelter wondering where you were."

I shook my head. "Mom, I wanted to hang out with my friends and see a baseball game. I'm the student body president. It's good to support the other kids. I can go to the shelter another time." I paused, gritting my teeth as I tried to formulate what I wanted to say and how to say it. "I know you're trying to look out for me, but I need some time to do what I want, when I want."

A long pause settled over the room, and from the lack of expression on her face, I was a little worried about what she was thinking. Had I just stood up to my mom to the point that she had nothing else to say in return?

"I agree," she said slowly, a smile spreading, highlighting her features. "There are some things we need to keep strict about, though. Don't plan anything for tomorrow night. I have something we need to do."

I groaned and then drained the rest of the water. "I hate it when you say that."

Her lips pinched, and her eyes flashed at me.

It wasn't worth the fight this late at night, and I just said, "Whatever," as I walked out of the room and trudged up the stairs.

My mind raced, trying to come up with something she could torture me with further. And on a Friday night no less.

I didn't have the brainpower right now to worry about it.

I lay down on my bed, swiping on my phone to scan the latest pictures from the people I followed on Quickstagram. Life looked so easy for some of these people, their parents giving them the freedom to come and go as they pleased. What would that be like?

CHAPTER 25

DAX

I was tired and groggy the next morning as I woke up for school, having gone to bed long past two in the morning.

When I reached for my phone, I saw a note on the floor next to me.

We headed out to school already. Figured you could sleep some more. See ya after. Karsten.

I checked the time on my phone, seeing I'd missed first period entirely. Jumping up, I ran and brushed my teeth. It took about five seconds to change clothes and throw a hat on before I grabbed my backpack and keys. Once inside the car, I turned the ignition and sped into reverse, adrenaline pumping through my system.

Mr. McKee hadn't mentioned anything about me missing classes in my punishment, but I wasn't going to challenge him on it. As much as it would've been nice to just skip the rest of the day, I had to get to class or risk having to sit the bench.

I was determined to graduate from Rosemont High. And even though I hadn't confessed my feelings for Kate, the thought of leaving made me even more determined to stick around.

After finding a parking spot near the back of the parking lot, I sprinted in, hearing the tardy bell ring above me. I turned right once I got to the commons and dashed down the hall, hoping I could slide into class without my math teacher realizing it.

"Daxton Stratton."

The voice caused me to freeze in the hall. I turned and saw Mr. McKee standing several feet away, arms folded tightly against his chest. His expression was a mixture of disappointment and frustration. I was in trouble.

"What are you doing out of class, young man?" If there was anyone who put the fear of a father into me, it would be that man.

"I, uh, I slept in on accident. Didn't hear my alarm. So I was just trying to get to math right now so I wouldn't miss too much."

The principal eyed me, long seconds passing as he waited to say anything. In the meantime, I could hear my teacher droning on inside the room, and I couldn't decide whether it was better to be out here or in there. Both were pretty torturous.

"Get to class, Stratton. Remember, you have to stay in line or you're done."

I didn't waste a moment before I stepped into the classroom, taking my seat near the back. I didn't need anything ruining my chances of graduating.

KATE

"Hey, how'd the game go last night?" I asked Dax when I walked into fourth period. He was sitting in a desk on the side of the room, and I took the seat in front of him.

He chuckled a bit. "We lost. Of course, when you aren't there, I actually hit a home run."

"Really?" I asked, my lips hurting from the wideness of my smile.

He nodded. "Yep. We ended up losing bad, though. I have to leave before this class ends for the next game. Are you coming tonight?"

I started nodding my head and then remembered my mom's appointment. "I have to do something with my mom tonight, but if we get done early, I'll definitely be there."

His expression fell a bit, and then he said, "We'll probably be playing a few games tomorrow, so you'll have to stop by then."

I laughed. "You kind of like having me come watch you, don't you?"

He gave me a coy side-smile and nodded. "It's nice to have

someone cheering for me. My siblings have their own things to get to, and since my grandma is older, she can't really drive to get there. With you there, I can tell the guys I have at least one person in my cheering section." His cheeks turned a rosy pink, and he glanced down at the top of the desk where someone had scratched the word "boring" into the surface.

"Well, I like watching you." I paused for a moment, trying to understand where he came from with that. I was so used to having my mother and stepdad at anything important that I forgot some students weren't as lucky.

We started class with Ms. Shiels up front trying to get our attention. There wasn't much to talk about since we'd finished the Harvest dance and the next big activity wasn't until we did the Christmas fundraiser at the end of November.

Soon enough, Dax stood to leave, and I was kind of sad I couldn't go with him. Now that I knew how much he cared about me at the games, a thrill ran through me. I'd never been truly needed in my life. Most people just took advantage of my willingness to help out and always just assumed I'd be there.

I had Dax on my mind the entire way home and was distracted as I tried to get some of my reading homework done. With whatever my mom had planned for the night and the possibility of going to Dax's games tomorrow, I wasn't sure how I'd get all the reading done for my English class if I didn't work on it now.

A knock came on the door about an hour later, the rhythm typical of my mom.

"Why aren't you ready?" she asked, glancing around the room. I'd thrown all the clothes I'd tried on that morning all over my bed and the floor. She picked up several pieces and walked to the closet, pulling out hangers. "You need to get going if you're going to be on time when he gets here."

My insides froze, my stomach beginning a low simmer. "Who gets here?"

"Trent Jacobs."

I frowned, grinding my teeth together. "Why would he be coming here? I thought you and I were supposed to do something together." I tilted my head to glare at her, not feeling her sudden meddling into my love life. Especially when she'd been getting mad at me for even thinking about having a relationship and dating Dax.

"I thought you could attend the Rosemont Fall Dinner together. Your stepdad can't make it because of work, and you can use our tickets and go in his place."

"I don't want to go with Trent, Mom. He's a tool." I spat out the last word, feeling it deep inside. Dax had never mentioned what Trent had said the day they'd gotten into a fight, but Serena had overheard someone say the fight started when Trent talked about Dax's mom being an outcast to the rich community because she'd married Dax's dad. If I'd have been in Dax's shoes, I would have punched him too.

"He's going to be here any minute. Just get dressed and go this one time for me, okay? It's just a little thing, but I would hate to see the tickets go to waste."

I bit the inside of my cheek, wishing I could just stay home and do nothing for the night. Or even better, head over to the baseball game and see Dax play again.

"I have homework." I glared at my mother, the one who thought grades and activities outweighed all things.

My mom laughed and shook her head. "It's a Friday night. You'll have plenty of time to do your homework tomorrow. Now get dressed right now or you won't be leaving this house until school on Monday."

I scowled, thinking that over. If I was stuck inside, I'd miss Dax's games. From the look on her face, there was no negotiating on this one.

"I'm going like this then," I said, falling onto my bed. I was dressed in a pair of Bermuda shorts and a light t-shirt that I'd just realized from looking down had a hole near the hem.

I heard hangers scraping along the metal closet rod and knew I wasn't going to get off that easy.

Her footsteps shuffled across my carpet over to my bed, and I closed my eyes, not in the mood to see what she'd chosen.

"Just put this on. We can work with your hair once you've done that."

Cloth brushed my arm, and when I opened my eyes, I was surprised to see one of the pieces from Serena and her mom's collection.

I sat up, surprised. "You chose one of Serena's pieces?" I stared at her, trying to close my mouth so the shock didn't show.

With a quick shrug, she gave me a small smile. "Whatever the girl lacks in propriety, she makes up for with her stylistic choices. Hurry up and get changed."

I wasn't sure what caused me to move into the closet and change: my mother semi-complimenting a girl she'd shunned the day before, or the haze I was in.

I'd bought the lacy shirt a couple weeks before but hadn't had a chance to wear it. It was definitely more fancy than school or the animal shelter would require. With a chambray color and a beaded neckline, it fit well.

I pulled on a cream pencil skirt and some wedges, preferring to not have to reenter my closet too many times in the next five minutes.

"Oh, Kate," my mother said, clapping her hands together and then covering her mouth for several seconds. "You look absolutely stunning. Trent is going to have a hard time taking his eyes off you."

Her comments threw me off, and the little high I'd felt at

being dressed up in new clothes disappeared. "What about not dating, Mom? Why is Trent allowed but Dax not?"

My mother refused to meet my eyes, fussing with the sleeves of my shirt. "I'm not saying you're dating Trent. But a guy can look even if you're not dating."

"What happened to not even looking at boys until I was in college? This is ridiculous!" Sourness invaded my mouth, and I thought about yelling more about all the inconsistencies in the "rules of the house" over the past few weeks. But I only had a few more months until graduation. I just hoped I'd hear back from some of the colleges on the border of Texas, or even in one of the surrounding states. If my relationship with my mother was going to survive, we needed more space.

And if I wanted to go to Dax's game, I had to suffer through this dinner.

The doorbell rang, and I froze. Did I really have to go on a non-date with Trent Jacobs?

CHAPTER 27

I'd sent a few texts to Kate the night before, but she didn't answer. It had been another late night when I got home from the game, and she was probably long asleep by that time.

So when I glanced at my phone Saturday morning, I grabbed it and turned on the screen, hoping she'd sent something that morning. My screen was empty, only a picture of my mom, Karsten, Bree, and me when we'd gone to a carnival a few years before she passed away.

I opened my message app anyway, hoping I'd missed something. After I reread the messages I sent her at midnight, I suddenly wished I could afford the newest phone that allowed you to see when people had seen the messages.

I'd gotten up earlier than I had the day before, which was good since we had another big game in a couple of hours. The smell of something cooking drew my attention, and I got out of the covers, stumbling to the kitchen.

"Bree, what are you making?" I asked, leaning against the doorframe.

"I was trying to make you some eggs. Karsten said today

is an important day for you, that all the college baseball scouts will be there watching." Her light-brown hair and pale-green eyes reminded me so much of my mother it hurt. She looked so innocent and as though she was waiting for a rebuke from me.

"Well, that's about the nicest thing anyone's done for me in a while." I walked up to her, reaching over her shoulder and sneaking a bit of scrambled egg. I savored it on my tongue. "That's pretty good, girl. Maybe you'll have to be the cook from now on."

She set the spatula down on the pan and waved her hands in front of me. "Now, now. I'm not that good. How hard is it to screw up eggs?"

I pulled out the chair next to the table across from her and grinned. "You'd be surprised." I leaned my head back against the wall, still trying to wake up. "How is cheer going, by the way?" It had been a while since I'd even talked to Kate or Bree about the dance classes, and since I hadn't gotten a text from Kate yet, might as well bring her up with my younger sister...

"I love cheerleading. It's so much fun, and I'm learning all the moves. Kate even said I'm catching up so fast." She beamed and started moving her hands in the way a cheerleader would do, clapping and stomping her feet.

A squeak came from down the hall, and Noni appeared in her wheelchair, her long white hair in a braid down the side of her face. When she had it like that, it usually meant she was feeling enough energy to get up and get going for the day. For me, that was a promising thing.

"Hello, my babies," she said, smiling weakly in our direction.

I jumped up and moved the chair away from the table so she could wheel up to it. "How are you feeling this morning, Noni?"

"Much better this morning, Daxton. Bree tells me you have some more baseball games today."

With a quick nod, I sat down again, drumming my fingers along the tabletop. "I do. We're in the semi-finals for this tournament, so we might have two games today." That usually meant a lot of kneeling in my catching gear, but it would be worth it if we could beat our rivals again.

"How's school going, young man?" This was the drawback to Noni feeling better, the constant questions about my life and decisions.

I nodded, staring over at Bree for a few seconds. "It's going really well, actually. I'm on Senior Committee and just trying to stay out of trouble."

She narrowed her eyes and pointed at me. "I better be seeing you walk across that stage. I'll have a picture of my oldest grandson in graduation attire, and the others when it's their time, of course," she said, glancing in Bree's direction. "That diploma is the most important thing right now, and I want your full attention on that."

I chuckled a bit. "I will, Noni. We've got a while left until graduation, but I'm keeping my grades up and doing well in baseball."

Bree brought over a plate of eggs and two pieces of toast that were a little darker than I usually liked. "Sorry, I forgot to turn the toaster down a notch. I'd make some others, but we're out of bread." She looked apologetic, reminding me of the afternoon after she'd gone shopping with Kate and realized we needed to pay her back.

I smiled, swiping my thumb across her chin. "This is perfect, Bree. I'm sure it will give me energy for the game."

"You'll impress those scouts," she said, stepping back to the stove and cracking more eggs into the pan.

After I swallowed a bite of egg, I turned to her, curious. "What makes you think I'm going to go to college? Noni over here thinks it will be a miracle if I make it through high school."

There were times when I forgot my sister was only eight years old, with the maturity in her coming out every once in a while. It was the first time in months that I hadn't seen her with the doll our mother had made her, dancing and singing with it like there was nothing in the world but that. The look in her eyes now was more sincere than I'd ever seen her.

"Because why not reach for the stars and see where you land?" She grinned before turning back around and scraping the eggs with the spatula.

"That's my girl," Noni said, purring. "Wise words, and ones I hope you'll take to heart, about everything."

I nodded, knowing I couldn't argue with either of them when I felt so inspired. I shoveled the rest of the eggs into my mouth and downed the toast, knowing I needed to get ready for my game. "Thanks again, Bree. That was the best breakfast I've had in a while."

"That's the *only* breakfast you've had in a while."

She had some truth there. I was usually running out the door before I got the chance to eat. Or leaving whatever was left for my siblings.

I dressed in my uniform, spraying a little cologne over me to mask the fact that I'd been too tired to wash it the night before. Hat on and bag packed, I said goodbye to Noni and Bree. Karsten would probably get up after I left.

Just another day of baseball ahead, and with the idea of college coaches and Kate possibly watching me, a kind of excitement and panic took over. Hopefully, it would turn out okay.

CHAPTER 28

KATE

I woke up Saturday morning with a glaring headache. The whole evening before had been one long, boring event, and I wished I'd told my mom I wouldn't go. But I'd survived, and I wasn't on lockdown Adams style, so I considered that and the fact I would get to see Dax today the only upsides.

Trent tried to be cool, but every time I looked at his face, I saw the guy who'd hit Dax and caused him to get in trouble.

Then again, that had been an advantage for me too, since I wouldn't have gotten to know him like I did now.

There were so many qualities about Rosemont's starting catcher that drew me to him, and I was pretty sure I was crushing on him. He wasn't the bad boy everyone had him pegged for, and he was the sweetest to his younger sister. The way he made me feel when I was around him, like I had all the choices in the world for what to do or who to be, made me like him that much more.

I leaned over and grabbed my phone, seeing a bunch of texts from Dax. My phone had died at dinner the night before, and I'd been too tired to wait long enough for it to turn on once I got home.

I smiled at the short messages he'd sent, even more excited to see him. I tapped the box to reply, hoping he'd be able to see the text before starting the game.

Good luck today! I should be there later!

I knew he was probably at the game already as they had to be there early for warmups.

It took a few minutes for me to find the energy to get out of bed, and then my head pounded, the pain behind my eyes making it difficult to see too far in front of me.

I lay back down, thinking a few more minutes of rest would help me recover.

An hour later, I woke back up, surprised that only some of the pain had ebbed, at least making it so the light from my window didn't cause a searing pain in my head anymore.

"Kate, what are you doing in bed still?" my mother asked, walking into my room. She had a basket of clothes on her hip and her hair swept up in a bun. That meant today was her deep cleaning day, something I wanted to avoid if possible. The level of clean she went to meant I would never get away for the games later today.

"I had a headache, so I went back to sleep for a bit."

"Can I get you an ibuprofen? Weren't you supposed to be somewhere this morning?"

My brain ticked through my mental schedule, and I couldn't remember having to be anywhere this early in the morning. "No, and even if I did, I need to rest. I'm exhausted."

My mother sat on the edge of the bed and studied my face, probably trying to see if I was telling the truth.

"Take today to rest. We have a lot going on tomorrow. The family is coming over for dinner, and it's been a while since we've seen them."

Hence the deep clean.

"Will do. I'm hoping to feel better later so I can go out."

"Out where?" she asked, her eyebrow raised in question.

"If the baseball team makes it to the championship game of the tournament, I want to be there…in support."

She scoffed, her nose turned up like she smelled Zane's shoes after a day outside. "It's not the season for baseball. What you should be doing is going to the fall lacrosse games, cheering for Trent."

I sat up, trying to ignore the pounding it caused. "Mom, stop pushing Trent. He's a jerk, and I don't want to talk about him or go on a date with him ever again."

The harsh tone in my voice caused us to both sit back in surprise.

"I thought you had a great time. Didn't you see the Quick-stagram picture of the two of you?" Of course, my mom would search and find anything related to me. I was barely on the picture-sharing app the past week, so the fact that there was a picture posted between last night and today was a surprise.

She pulled out her phone and tapped the screen a couple of times, my insides squeezing as I expected the worst.

"Here," she said, handing her phone over to me.

I glanced down at the picture. It was posted by Trent only minutes after he dropped me off with the caption of "Best night ever!"

In the picture, I sat several inches away from him, my face pinched in a half-smile. He'd just said something totally inappropriate about some of the people there, and I was over the whole date thing.

"Mom, I don't even look happy here." I pointed to the screen and handed it back to her.

She lifted the phone to her face and squinted, not having her glasses on at the time. "You look happy there. How was it? You got in later, and I was just happy you made it home safely."

Not to mention she hadn't cared about curfew for the first time ever.

"Like I said, I don't want to go on any more setup activities with him." The thought of his hug when he dropped me off on my doorstep last night, his hand trying to drift to areas off limits, made me cringe even now. It fueled me, and I looked straight at my mother, ready to be done with everything that had bugged me for a long while.

"I'm not doing a hundred activities anymore, Mom. I'll keep one and then still teach at the studio, but I need to breathe, need the freedom to relax when I want to, to have a life of my own. I'll get into a college, but I don't want to major in business. I want to study art, all the facets and types. I know that will disappoint you, but I'm done. I just can't keep up that kind of schedule, nor do I want to anymore."

The emotions played across her face, the flicker of anger, hurt, and finally disappointment.

She stood, not saying a word as she left the room, shutting the door behind her.

Guilt pulsed through me, and the silence between us felt like a chasm. But for the first time in my life, I didn't go running out the door to appease her. It had been so long since I'd stood up to her that I had to hold out strong, had to tell myself all would be okay in the end, even if it didn't feel so now.

She'd done a lot in my life to control the path I would go on, but something about her forcing me to go on a date with the slimeball of Rosemont High when she didn't want me to date anyone caused my eyes to burn with a surge of tears.

I was done playing that game.

Pulling out my laptop, I pulled up the websites of my favorite art-focused colleges and began the application process. It didn't matter if I got into one of the business schools. I was going to do what was right for me and would make me happy.

I hadn't done anything outright bad, but in my mother's eyes, I'd just burned the house down.

CHAPTER 29

DAX

The game had been a nail-biter, and adrenaline still pulsed through me minutes after the game finished. We'd managed to pull off the win of the semi-final game, and I couldn't have been more excited. Now I just needed to prep myself to catch for Ben in the next game since his pitches were much different and faster than Tony's.

The team sat under a tree, trying to take advantage of the little shade at the ballpark, waiting for the next game to finish so we'd know who we were playing.

Someone's mom had brought a bag of sliced oranges, and we were downing them like we hadn't had something so good in a long while.

"Are Penny and Serena coming to the next game?" Nate asked Jake and Ben between bites of his orange.

"Serena is," Ben said, a slight grin on his face.

"Penny has her own tourney. I think I'll see her later tonight, though. They were set to play the number-one competition team in the state this afternoon, so we'll see if they can pull it off." Jake scanned the field, watching as one of the players hit a double into left center field. "Like us, of course."

"Well, it doesn't look like Dax's girlfriend will be making it today," Colt said, lifting his phone. I was too far away to see what it was, just seeing the logo of the Quickstagram app.

"She's not my girlfriend," I said, wishing she really was. We'd made so much progress and had so much fun over the past few weeks that the hope grew stronger each time we were together. I just needed to suck up my pride and ask her out.

The guys started making noises that sounded bad, and then I scooted forward, taking the phone from Colt.

The picture on the screen hit me in the chest like a dagger to the heart, and even though I had a group of guys around me, I couldn't just shrug it off and not study it further.

Kate sat next to Trent Jacobs, looking beautiful with a white shirt and her hair up, the smile on her face hurting even worse. When did she go out with him?

I glanced down at the caption of the photo and saw he'd posted it last night, saying it had been the best night ever.

Was that what she'd been doing with "her mom"? Going out with the guy who had the moral compass of a snail?

I shoved the phone back at Colt, feeling the rising anger build in my chest.

"You'll be all right," Jake said, tapping me on the back. "Penny thought she saw me making out with some other girl. There's got to be some explanation there."

"We're not dating, Jake. She can date whoever she wants." I stood, feeling stifled underneath the shade with everyone staring at me, pity in their expressions.

Walking away from the group, I strode over to the bathrooms, needing a few moments of peace.

I'd been holding out hope, but I should never have let myself believe I could be in a relationship with Kate Adams.

The most amazing girl at Rosemont High who would just date people from her own social class. I was just the pity date.

I made a fist and went to punch the cinderblock wall of the bathroom, stopping only an inch or two away from the wall. I didn't need to screw up my chances of winning the next game by breaking my hand.

I would just have to get rid of the feelings I had for Kate, put up a wall every time I saw her and make sure she didn't worm her way back into my life. Not that she'd want to. I was just a boy from a trailer park. Not worthy of her love.

CHAPTER 30

KATE

My mom had left to run some errands, and I snuck out while she was gone, grateful the headache had finally disappeared so I could think and drive more clearly.

I drove to the field, excited to see Dax, and I just hoped he would do well in the game.

Pick me up for the game? Serena asked in a text.

I'd already pulled into the parking lot, but I turned around, grateful her house wasn't too far away from the fields. I didn't even have to honk once I arrived before she slid into the passenger seat.

"What happened to your car?" I asked, shifting the car into reverse.

Serena groaned. "I might have gotten into a little accident yesterday, and now the front wheel won't drive. It's back in the shop."

I stepped on the brake, giving her a once-over. "Are you all right? You didn't get any injuries, did you?"

Serena's face was a sheepish grin. "No injuries. Just hurt

pride. I ran into a cement pole down at the mall last night. Let's just say my dad laughed and tried to scold me for it."

"Sounds about right," I said, driving back to the field.

"What did you do last night?" she asked, more curiosity in her face than normal. That meant she knew something.

I parked near a shaded tree and leaned my head back against the headrest. "Ugh, my mother set me up on a date/non-date with Trent Jacobs. It was pure torture. We had to go to the dinner they have here in Rosemont, and we were the youngest people there."

"You looked kind of cozy in the picture Trent posted." The last few words held a hint of a question, and a measure of panic formed in my stomach.

Raising my hands, I said, "I'm telling the truth, girl. I'm not excited about the fact that I had to put up with Trent the Jerk for a whole evening, but I'm even more annoyed at my mother for telling me I couldn't date all my life, and then when I'm showing interest in someone she doesn't approve of, she arranges a date for me."

Serena cringed and nodded. "Yeah, that sounds awful. So, do you like Dax, then?" Leave it to her to be so straight-forward.

Blowing out a breath, I nodded slowly. "Yes, I do like him. He's a good guy, only trying to do what he can to help out his family. And he treats me like I matter, and that my opinions count for something."

"Could he be the Masked Kisser?" Her eyebrows were raised, and she looked thoughtful.

I shook my head, trying to think that one through. "What makes you think that?"

"I don't know. From everything you've said, I was thinking it could be him, not some guy who went to another school. I've heard Ben talk about a masked guy a couple of times, and I'm thinking it's Dax, Nate, or Colt."

I turned to stare out at the baseball field, trying to replay the memory in my head. The details were getting fuzzier as time went by, with the physical features of the guy fading away. The only thing that hadn't changed was the tingling sensation in my lips every time I thought about the kiss.

I pulled the keys out of the ignition and stepped out of the car. As exciting as the thought was, if Dax had been the Masked Kisser, he would have told me, right? We'd shared so much in the past few weeks that I was sure we had that level of trust.

As we walked over to the stands, the guys were all out warming up, taking grounders and pop flies. I looked around for the pitcher and saw Ben throwing in a small fenced-off section. The bullpen, I think it was?

Directly opposite him was Dax, and I walked up to the fence and whispered, "Hey!"

He turned to look at me, his eyes narrowing once he recognized me. "Hey."

I wasn't sure if it was just that he had his catcher's mask on or if he wasn't supposed to talk to me right now that made the tone of his voice sound so short.

I waved and stepped away from the fence, my stomach turning. I followed Serena up to the stands, and we took a seat in the shade. It was a nice break from the Texas heat, even this late in the fall.

"Well, that greeting didn't go very well," I mumbled, trying not to cry.

"Trent did post that picture on Quickstagram, Kate. Maybe it's gotten to Dax by now."

Everything inside me clenched at the thought. If that were the case, what would he be thinking? That I'm some girl who says she can't stand a guy and then goes out with him? That made it seem like I wasn't being honest, and I didn't like that.

Maybe it would have been better if I'd stayed home today.

* * *

THE GAME WAS EXCITING, with plenty of actions to help distract my overactive analytical brain. Dax missed a ball at one point, having to run back and get it as one of the runners advanced to the next base. He didn't hit very well either, getting out the few times he was up to bat. The last at-bat, he swung on the third strike, ending the game. I expected him to throw his helmet and start yelling, but he just shook his head and walked back to the dugout, filing out with his team to congratulate the opponents.

I hadn't seen Penny arrive, but she was already at the fence line, waiting for the guys to come in, dressed in her softball uniform.

"How'd it go today?" I asked, leaning against the chain-link fence next to her.

"About the same as here, it looks like." Penny took losing hard, and I could tell she was mulling it over.

The guys started filing out after the award ceremony, and my heart pounded, hoping Dax would understand about last night if he'd already seen the picture.

Jake and Ben walked up to their girlfriends and hugged them while Dax waved goodbye and started walking out of the complex.

"Dax, wait. You're not even going to say hi, or thanks for coming?" I asked, jogging behind him.

"Hi," he said, turning around. "Thanks for coming." His voice was so low and monotone that I was more irritated than anything.

I ran in front of him, putting out my hand to stop him. "Dax, why are you being like this?"

"We're not dating, Kate, and it's obvious you don't have

feelings for me if you're going out with Trent Jacobs. Thanks for coming, and I'll see you at school." He pushed past me, not hard enough to knock me over, but enough to let me know how frustrated he was.

I watched his back as he walked away, and before I knew it, the words were out of my mouth. "Are you my Masked Kisser?"

He stopped, his posture stiff and his hands clenching and unclenching. When he didn't turn around, I ran to stand in front of him to see his face.

He kept his eyes straight ahead, not glancing down at me.

"Are you the guy who kissed me at the party last spring?" I reached out and touched his arm, which seemed to break him out of his trance.

His eyes bored into mine, and his jaw ground back and forth for a minute. "What if it *was* me?" he asked in a soft whisper. "It's not like it would matter. There's no way your mom would let us go out, and it seems you've already found yourself another guy. I wish you luck with that."

"What do you mean, what if it was you? Why wouldn't you tell me?" I pushed against his arm, anger surging. I was so sick of people treating me like I didn't know any better about what I needed in my life. And I was sick of following other people's plans for what I should be doing.

"It was me." He broke his gaze away and walked out into the parking lot. His stride showed a measure of exhaustion and defeat.

I wanted to go after him, but at this point, it was probably better that I just leave him alone and push all thoughts of Daxton Stratton out of my life. He couldn't trust me with a small secret, one that I considered to be huge. And he also didn't know me well enough if he assumed I'd gone on a date with Trent Jacobs.

As much as I told myself it wouldn't hurt to let him go, I

needed to steel myself against the fact that it would all work out in the end.

An arm wrapped around my shoulders, and I turned to see Penny giving me a sad smile. "You found your Kisser, huh?"

I nodded, my chin wobbling as I tried to keep from crying. "Yeah." I wiped away a tear that had broken free. "Why didn't he tell me it was him?" He could've easily told me when we were designing our shirts. I had been one of the three people he'd kissed after all.

"Maybe he was worried you wouldn't like him. He's been through a lot in his life, and rejection might not go over well for him."

"But he didn't even give me that chance to decide."

Penny shook her head and took a few steps forward. "Who can understand guys some times?" She gave me a hug before we got into our cars and headed out.

I glanced around the parking lot, hoping I'd catch a glimpse of Dax and that he'd come apologize. But the parking lot was nearly empty.

CHAPTER 31

DAX

I drove around for a bit, ending up at the garage because I didn't want to go home just yet. That morning I'd left the trailer with such hope that I had a future ahead of me, that I had a chance with an amazing girl and there was a possibility of college in my future. With the way I played today and my hurt over seeing Trent and Kate together, I just needed to disappear for a while.

"What are you doing here?" Doc asked, wiping down his hands. The towel he was using had just as much grease on it as his hands, and I didn't think it was making much of a difference.

"Just needed a distraction."

"After a baseball game? That's a new one from you."

I shook my head, trying not to give in to his small joke. "I just saw a picture of the girl I like with the guy who got me into the whole probation mess in the first place."

"Ahhh, girl trouble. That is usually a distraction in itself." He rested his hands on the tool table, staring at me with a small smile. "What are you going to do about it?"

"I'm not going to do anything. I'm a kid from a different

neighborhood, different social class than she is. How in the world could I even think I have a chance with her?"

Doc grinned, and I knew I wasn't going to like what he said next. "I seem to remember another girl from the same area of town falling in love with a rough kid, settling down, and having three kids, all of whom are great in their own right. Her love story ended shorter than planned, but she always loved your father and did everything she could to make things work for you three."

At the mention of my angel mother, my throat constricted, a large mound filling the space there.

"Yeah, but I have absolutely nothing to offer Kate Adams. She's already got the world at her fingertips. Why would she need me?"

"That's something you'll have to figure out, young Dax," Doc said, chuckling. "Love is a crazy thing, but if you like her enough, maybe she's worth the risk. Have you told her how you feel?"

I glanced down, hitting my shoe against the raised crack in the concrete floor several times. "No." I'd admitted to the kiss last spring, but that didn't translate to how I felt now.

Doc shrugged. "That would be the best place to start. She'll never know unless you tell her how you feel, and you'll be able to figure out your future once you do."

I nodded, knowing he made sense but still not feeling brave enough to put myself out there like that. She hadn't said anything about the kiss, whether she liked it or not, and I wasn't sure I could take another disappointment right now.

"Thanks, Doc. I should probably get home."

"You sure you don't want to work on this car with me?" he asked, holding out a wrench. "You did drive out here for a reason, right?"

I considered the offer and stepped forward, first grabbing one of the old aprons Doc never bothered to wear. After I tied it around my uniform, I took the tool from him and listened to what he'd already done on the car. This was the distraction I needed, focusing on a problem I could see and fix.

I'd deal with everything on Monday. For now, I was just going to make it through the weekend.

CHAPTER 32

DAX

Monday seemed to take longer to pass than it should have. I was grateful I didn't have Senior Committee as I still wasn't ready to face Kate. The hurt in her eyes haunted me for most of the weekend. Would telling her I was the guy who'd kissed her have made a difference? Would it have made it so she didn't go on a date with Trent?

We were congregated in the commons during lunch. I'd used some of my money to buy a slice of pizza from the cafeteria, knowing I needed to finish the rest of the school day and not having a growling stomach would help that. It was November, and I'd already started counting down the days to graduation.

The bell rang, and we started down the halls, breaking apart to go in different directions for our classes.

"Hey, Stratton," said a familiar voice behind me.

I turned to see Trent striding up to me.

"I had such a great time with your girl on Friday. I think I'll ask her out again for this week."

I ground my teeth together and focused on keeping my

hands at my sides. Students filed past us, some stopping to watch the scene unfold.

"I'm thinking I could take her somewhere a bit more intimate," he said, grinning. The next words out of his mouth had my skin crawling, lewd comments about what he'd do to her.

Before I could restrain myself, my fist flew up and slammed into his jaw, sending his head snapping back.

His hand raised to touch the spot where I'd hit him, and his devilish smile returned. "Just wait, Stratton. You'll be expelled before the day is through."

Instead of fighting me like I thought he would, he turned and walked down the hall toward the principal's office. So much for graduating with my friends here at Rosemont.

KATE

Buzz was all I could interpret when I walked into my eighth-period class. I'd been delayed getting back from lunch as I had to run an errand for Ms. Shiels, and the hallways had already been cleared when I walked into the building.

I took a seat next to Melissa, one of my student body officers, and whispered, "What's going on?"

She turned to me, her eyes raised to her hairline. "You don't know?"

"Know what?" I glanced around the room, trying to piece it all together.

It had been a rough weekend as it was, with the whole Dax thing going down. My chest still hurt much more than it should have with us hanging out for less than three weeks. But I still liked the boy, liked the fact that he was my Mystery Kisser. But I didn't know how to approach the subject again. He was already mad about the Trent Jacobs date night, so how was I going to get past that betrayal?

"There was a fight," Melissa began.

"Dax and Trent," the blond-haired sophomore girl in front of Melissa chirped in.

Jeff, behind me, piped up. "It was epic. Dax threw a punch like you wouldn't believe. I was sure Trent was going to have some kind of neck issues after that one."

My mind swirled with all the information, and I couldn't figure out my own emotions. Dax hit Trent again? That meant he was in big trouble. Like, bigger than just the normal. Would Mr. McKee expel him? A pit formed in my stomach, and I wanted to find him and make sure he was okay.

"Why did he hit him?" I asked.

The group went silent for several moments before Melissa looked at me and said, "Because of you."

"What? Dax is mad at me for a lot of things right now." I was trying to see which side was rooting for me. Knowing Trent's awful sense of humor, I was hoping it was Dax who had punched him in defense of me for something.

"Because Trent was saying some pretty awful stuff about you, demeaning stuff, like you were just a trophy on his arm and what he would do to you and stuff like that. Dax tried to hold back but ended up landing a punch to Trent's right cheek." Melissa bobbed her head. She must have seen the whole thing.

"I can't wait to see how that black eye turns out," Jeff said, a giddy laugh coming from him.

As much as I disliked Trent, that seemed a bit harsh. "That's not something we should be happy about."

Jeff shrugged, and the teacher stood at the front of the class, ready to instruct us on science. My brain spun, and as each moment passed, I got more and more excited that Dax had actually punched someone for me. For me, Kate Adams. I had a lot of people who liked me and helped me with things, but I'd never had someone go to such lengths to defend me.

My hand shot into the air, and I waved it around, trying to get my teacher's attention.

"Yes, Ms. Adams?" he said, his voice sounding ornery since I'd interrupted his lecture.

"May I use the hall pass?" It was about the only way the guy would let me leave. If I said I had to go rescue the guy I had a major crush on, I'd definitely get turned down for that one.

"I really have to go, sir," I said, giving him a grimace.

"You were already late to this class."

"Please, please?"

When he shook his head, the scariest thing I'd done in a while was stand up and dash out the door.

"You'll get a truancy, Miss Adams," he called down the hall behind me.

At that point, I didn't care. I didn't need a perfect record for citizenship if I could save Dax from being expelled altogether from our school.

My footsteps echoed through the halls, and I ran around to the side of the office, pushing open the door and trying to catch my breath.

"Is he in there?" I asked the secretary, pointing to the principal's office.

"Yes, but I wouldn't go in there just now. He's in a disciplinary meeting."

Probably with Dax.

I stepped forward and opened the door, and the surprise on Dax's face was priceless.

"Is there something you need, Miss Adams?" Mr. McKee asked, his lips pursed and eyes flashing. "We're in the middle of a disciplinary meeting."

"That's what I came to talk to you about, sir," I said, glancing between him and Dax a couple of times as I shut the door behind me. Dax's eyebrows drew together like he couldn't believe I was doing this.

"Go on," Mr. McKee said, waving his hand in my direction.

I blew out a breath, now avoiding looking in Dax's direction as nerves crept into my stomach and chest. "I've gotten to know Dax over the past few weeks. He's been working so hard toward graduation, trying to stay out of trouble and doing everything he can to graduate from Rosemont. If there is someone you should blame for the fight today, it's Trent Jacobs."

Mr. McKee's face showed curiosity, and I continued on, the words tumbling out in the process.

"Trent said some derogatory things about me, and Dax was only trying to defend me." I turned to look at Dax, giving him a grateful smile.

"How did you know that?" Dax asked, the corner of his mouth turned up a few centimeters.

"Several people in my eighth-period class confirmed it. I got in late because I was grabbing some supplies for Ms. Shiels, and when I got back, it was all my class could talk about."

"So there were more witnesses?" Mr. McKee asked, his fingers interlocked and his elbows resting on the desk.

"Yes, sir," I said, nodding.

Mr. McKee nodded. "Okay, Miss Adams. Wait outside."

I glanced back in Dax's direction, hoping my intervention had helped somewhat. He gave me a small smile, his eyes boring into mine as I closed the door.

"Kate, what are you doing here? Aren't you supposed to be in class?"

I turned to face my mother, taking a moment to breathe as the courage I'd had upon leaving my class built again.

"I'm here to defend Dax," I said, straightening my shoulders, trying to look a little more confident than I felt.

"Why?"

"Because I like him and he's a really good guy. After all I've been through this year, he defended me when Trent was spreading lies today. I would think that deserves some praise." My mouth clamped shut as anger took over. Why was she so hard on people with their imperfections?

She rested her hand on her hip and moved toward me. "Trent did that to you?"

I nodded. "I'm pretty sure if you found out the truth from Dax's previous fight with Trent, you'd see he was the start of that problem as well."

My mother glanced toward the closed door and then back at me before stepping forward and wrapping her arms around me. "I'm so sorry, Katie Bug. I didn't know."

The use of my childhood nickname brought tears to my eyes. It had been so long since she'd called me that, and the tender way she'd said it made me want to curl up and hide away for a few days after this was all over. It had been scary to challenge the authority of my teacher and then charge into the principal's office, but I'd risk the fallout. As long as Dax was given a chance to stay, it would all be worth it.

"I'm sorry I pushed you to date him. And I'm sorry I didn't give Dax a chance."

I pulled away, wiping at a few stray tears, and nodded. "I try not to lie to you, Mother, but I wish you'd let me make my own decisions. I need to be able to have room to breathe, have time to decide what is best for myself."

Her eyes searched my face for several seconds, and she reached forward, tucking some hair behind my ear. "And where do you suggest we start?"

I blew out a breath, surprised that she was actually listening to me on this. "I don't want to study business or be a lawyer. I want to study art or graphic design. Those are the things that I love, and I haven't been doing enough of them. I just want to make sure I'm living my own life, not the one you've picked out for me to shield me from what could happen in the future."

"But I wasn't doing that," my mom said, looking like I'd just slapped her. The urge to take it all back crept up as the people pleaser in me tried to take over again.

"But that's how it feels. I get why you did it, but I'm telling you now that I don't want to do it anymore. I'll keep one or two volunteer activities, but I need to have some time to spend with my friends, to go do things that normal teenagers do. I'll be an adult soon enough."

For the first time in several years, I saw my mom's eyes water, and she sniffed, glancing away. "You're right. You only get to be a teenager once, and I've been trying to heap responsibilities on you as though I could take away all the pain I went through when I lost your dad."

She pulled me in for a hug again, and this time it felt like it did before my father died, the comfort of a safe place where I didn't have to have my guard up all the time, worrying about what I said or did around her.

Pulling back enough to see her face, I said, "Mom, I really like Dax. I might even be falling in love with him." I raised a finger when she opened her mouth. "I know I might not exactly know what love is, but after everything I've learned about him, he's one of the most amazing people I've ever met. He'd do anything for his siblings and his family, and he's smarter than I am at math and science. Will you just let me see how things go?"

She ran her fingers through my hair and then mumbled against the top of my head, "I think I can do that."

"Did you really mean that?" a deep voice behind me asked.

I let go of my mom and turned to find Dax standing a few feet from us, his hands in his pants pockets and looking more vulnerable than I'd ever seen him. He didn't appear to have any bruises or cuts like the last fight.

"Mean what?" I asked softer than I expected.

"What you just told your mom. That you like me?" The corners of his mouth twitched as if he was more nervous than I'd been to tell my mother all that.

I stepped away from my mom and walked closer to him. "Yes, I meant it all."

My mom walked forward, her attention on Dax. "I'm sorry I judged you unfairly. I knew your mother, and she was a great woman. I should've known she would've raised someone as amazing as you. Thank you for defending my daughter. It was my fault she was with him Friday night to begin with. She didn't want to go."

Dax swallowed and nodded, looking as though he couldn't get the words out. He finally choked out, "I'd do it again, ma'am."

My mom waved and then walked away down the hall, leaving the two of us standing in the empty hallway.

Dax reached forward and took my hands, causing the most intense shock to pass through my body. He must have felt it too because we chuckled together.

"Kate Adams, I've liked you for a long time, and I guess I didn't tell you about the kiss because I wanted to hold on to some twisted fairy tale that you could like me back. I've always been afraid of being rejected, that I wouldn't be good enough for anyone, and I knew that even if you couldn't be with me, I didn't want anyone to ruin your reputation."

I slid my arms around his waist and leaned my head on his chest. "And that's why I like you so dang much, Daxton Stratton. You have honor that no one ever gives you credit for. Social status and reputation are the last things on my mind because I know the you behind all the rumors. All I want is to be happy." I paused for several seconds and then looked up at him. "So, Masked Kisser, do you want to be my boyfriend?"

The widest grin I'd ever seen crossed his face, and he laughed. "Yes, I do. More than I've wanted anything in a long time."

He dipped his head down and captured my lips with his, that same energy from the party last spring even stronger this time around. The bell rang, and students milled around us, oohing and aahing.

Dax pulled back and leaned his forehead against mine. "We should probably get out of the way."

I wrapped my arms around his neck and pulled him back down for another kiss. "Nah, I've been waiting a long time for this."

EPILOGUE

DAX

It was spring, and it seemed like my life had changed so much over the past six months. Kate was the best thing that had ever happened to me, and I knew I always had her in my corner.

When I first introduced her to my dad, I saw a hint of the old guy he'd been while my mother was alive, and he'd only improved since then. He'd taken a local trucking job so he could be home whenever the kids got home from school, and we did a lot more together. Noni was still alive and doing well, one of the things I'd hoped for since Mr. McKee allowed me to stay enrolled at Rosemont High.

Kate's mother changed a lot as well, allowing Kate to pursue some graphic design classes the local college offered online. She also warmed up to me, liking the fact that I could reach things she couldn't when her husband wasn't around.

And here I stood in the hall of the high school, dressed in a cap and gown, waiting for them to call out my name. I walked along the stage as my name came across the speakers, shaking hands and accepting my diploma from Mr. McKee.

"Well done, Dax. I'm sure your grandmother is proud."

I nodded, glancing out past the bright lights of the stage and focusing on my little section of fans. I could barely see my father's face, but it looked like he was crying. "Yes, sir. My whole family is."

"Congratulations, son. I wish you all the best."

The announcer called the name of the student behind me, and I turned to walk off the other side of the stage. Kate was waiting for me there, and I pulled her in to give her a small kiss, my excitement that we were finally there making this moment even sweeter.

"What a day, huh?" she said, wrapping an arm around my waist as we headed down to the chairs left open for students in the auditorium.

I chuckled. "Yep. We finally made it. Now on to the rest of our lives."

"Well, at least college. When do you have to be at Texas A&M?" She beamed up at me, still so proud that I'd secured a scholarship to play baseball there.

"Not until after Labor Day. What about design school?"

"Same. That means we have the whole summer together." She wrapped her other arm around my waist, pulling in to hug me.

"Then let's make it the best summer yet."

Six months earlier, I didn't think my life was worth much, that the people in it didn't care whether I succeeded or failed, but I was wrong. And now I had an amazing girlfriend, my father was a father again, and I had the opportunity to play the sport I loved in college. What could be better than all that?

* * *

Keep reading for a sneak peak of Meg and Parker's story in
Love, Austen

* * *

Thank you for reading *Love, Austen!* If you enjoyed it, I would
love to see a review from you. You can also subscribe to
Britney's newsletter here:
Subscribe to Britney's List
Or join her Facebook Reader Group

CHAPTER 1

LOVE, AUSTEN

*M*eg Austen heard the computer humming its startup song as she sorted the envelopes at her desk. A couple of pieces of junk mail and several bills. Twisting a piece of her blond hair, she considered leaving the envelopes untouched. Maybe if she blinked fast enough, they'd disappear. She loved to see what came in the mailbox as a kid, but now she understood that with the postman usually came papers demanding money, a never-ending battle.

She didn't have to open the letters to know what they said. Past-Due in red ink. The costs of remodeling and renting a physical building weren't things she'd had to worry about before, but her growing matchmaking business had stretched her bank account thinner than she'd ever seen it. Ramen noodles was a staple in her apartment now.

One envelope stood out from the pile, its square shape sticking up next to the rest. These were the letters she wanted to receive. The ones printed on linen or parchment or mylar, the words in an elegant script. Pulling the sharp letter opener from her desk drawer, she sliced open the envelope and pulled out the contents.

Meg skimmed past the names of the bride's parents to find Rebecca Ann spelled out in a swoopy script. Her husband-to-be was Richard Story, one of the three matches Meg had picked out for her. Included was a picture of the happy couple sitting on a park bench, gazing into each other's eyes.

This. Everything about this validated why she did what she did. That look on his face as he stared at her. Rebecca's wide smile. Totally worth the hours of research it took to compile the data to find people their best match.

She stood, turning to the wall at her right. Covering the wall were dozens of invitations with the engagement pictures taped next to them. The success stories of the Love, Austen Matchmaking Company over the past four years.

A sharp pain sliced through her chest, envy trickling in its wake. Her life was better than she could have hoped, near perfect by certain standards. She owned a business she adored, had amazing friends, and all the Nutella hot chocolate she could drink from the creperie around the corner from the new building.

The only thing she was missing was the kind of relationship her best friend Lily had with her fiancé, Ben. With their wedding on the horizon, Meg's life would change, as she'd depended on Lily for so many things. Marriage changed friendships and while she had been trying to prepare herself for it over the past several months, she could only hope she'd find peace from it all.

Taping the newest invitation to the wall, she glanced at the envelopes again, knowing she'd have to tackle them before lunch, or they'd sit there for weeks. She arranged them on the corner of her desk and clicked on her email inbox. Several new emails from current and potential clients waited and as she scanned the headlines, her eyes stopped on one of them.

Her stomach did a flip as she read: INVESTMENT REQUEST. With a quick click, she scrolled down faster than she could even comprehend. She hadn't learned anything from her attempt at speed reading and rolled the page back to the top.

"Dear Miss Austen,

We thank you for your application to the Boston Investors Alliance. We have gone through your profile and request more information about your company before moving forward."

Not one to object to reading the end of a book, her eyes slid to the last paragraph.

"Please give our office a call between 9:00 am–5:00 pm in the next day or two. Ask for Mark Allred."

Her hand hovered over the receiver as she stared at the wall in front of her.

Should I call them now?

She scanned to see what time they sent the email. Forty-seven minutes ago. Was that too soon to respond? Would they think she was desperate?

What was a little humiliation? It had almost killed her pride to send in the application in the first place. She'd made a goal to depend on herself for any need, business or other-wise, the day she found out her mother had taken half of her college savings.

After a coaxing debate from her assistant Tiffany, she'd decided that getting a business loan, or taking on investors, wasn't like robbing a bank. Besides, people had the guts to convince investors on TV that their product would make millions. Sending in an electronic application made her grateful she didn't have to beg and plead in front of an audience.

Nervous energy bubbled in her stomach, and she shook her hands to calm herself for a moment.

They can say no. I'll just find another way to do things. Just breathe.

She picked up the phone, dialing the number at the bottom of the email.

"Boston Investors Alliance. How may I direct your call?" a woman's voice came over the line.

"Um… that's a good question." The name already escaped her, and she had to skim the email, seeing the information she needed, "May I speak to Mark Allred, please?"

"One moment, please."

Meg heard the click, and then that awful trumpet, trying-to-be-jazz type music filled her ears. She pulled the phone away and rolled her eyes. If they were going to play music, why couldn't they play something most people listened to?

Once the call connected, the ringing tone echoed in Meg's ear, sending her mind into doubt. She'd gained experience with talking to people of various economic backgrounds in the time she'd been running Love, Austen, but the thought of some unknown person deciding whether to give her money based on a few questions from an application formed knots in her stomach.

Her finger hovered over the disconnect button, giving herself to the count of ten. When she reached eight, a male voice answered, causing her mind to scramble as it focused on his words. Her stomach gurgled, and dryness overtook her mouth.

Chocolate. She'd need some of that when this call finished.

After quick introductions, the raspy voice on the line said, "I'm looking at your file now. With all the information of your background, your business plan, and everything else you've submitted, you've passed the first stage of the process. We feel it's important to vet each client before handing out money." He paused and Meg hoped it wasn't to drive the point home. She wasn't giving up now. "The board requested a phone interview, to discover why you want people to invest in your company. There's only so much we can learn on paper."

The line went silent, and Meg pursed her lips, unsure what to do. Was he waiting for her to answer? Or was this another pause? Her heart raced, and she placed a hand over it, hoping to calm it enough to breathe in a few mouthfuls of air without sounding like she'd just run a 5K.

"Well, sir, I've been working on Love, Austen since my senior year of college, so almost five years. In that time, we've been able to grow our clientele each year, this last year by nearly thirty-three percent, many coming from referrals of past clients. Our success rate of couples still together after the first year has been steady for most of that time and in the last year, rose another six percent."

Mr. Allred said nothing. Twisting the cord at the base of her receiver, Meg tried not to breathe loudly into it.

"What would our investment go toward?"

She visualized the online application where she'd detailed her answer to that exact question. Closing her eyes, she said, "Well, sir, we've just opened our first physical location on Beacon Street, giving us the adequate room for meeting potential clients as well as bringing in some of the locals. But my overall vision for this company is to go global. After meeting with a business analyst, he suggested we increase our online footprint. My priority is to design an app allowing people to benefit from all the conveniences of our company from anywhere around the world."

"Ah, those applications my grandkids talk about. I'm

lucky I know how to text. Don't get me started about those smiley faces." The man chuckled, and a pity laugh escaped from her lips.

Great. My future rests in the hands of a man who doesn't understand technology. It was the very basis of her business in the way she calculated personality traits and compatibility scores to match her clients. She tried to picture the man, probably nearing retirement at a job he'd held for at least forty years. Comfort was his signature.

The thought sparked an idea and she said, "Yes, but we want to make it user-friendly. Something people can use no matter their skill level with technology. We match couples from age eighteen up as high as eighty so far. We at Love, Austen believe that everyone should have a chance at love, and for some, even a second."

The man let out a sigh. "That's a great sentiment, and I'm interested to see the inner-workings of your business. My question for you, Miss Austen, is how much do you trust in your matching program?"

"Excuse me?"

"Do you have a boyfriend, husband, or significant other?"

She opened her mouth but found the air too thick to swallow. The closest thing to a boyfriend was the stock photo in the silver frame Tiffany had given her for her last birthday. Her family was almost non-existent, and her life was her business, making it difficult for picture-worthy moments.

"Boyfriend? I have a… boy-friend." She smacked herself on the forehead, hoping he hadn't heard it. Liquid slurping echoed from the other end, and she frowned. She was sweating over a simple word, and he was smacking his lips in her ear.

Mr. Allred cleared his throat and said, "Perfect. We look forward to meeting him."

Another pause on the line sent Meg's mind into overdrive. What had she been thinking? Did they expect her to run all the numbers and matching for said boyfriend as well? She pictured some men she'd met wanting to be matched in the last few months and found herself cringing to think of even holding their hands.

Sound came from the other line again, pulling her back to the present. "For our company to get an overall picture of your business, we will be sending someone to look at the place, your processes, and any other details we might need to consider. If you have any special events coming up, please notify our office. Client experiences are valuable to the final decision, and we weigh those considerably higher than the basic information. We hope to have an answer to you in the next thirty days."

"You'll come to my office?" Why was her brain moving in slow motion?

"Yes, like I said before, we like to get the overall picture rather than just the numbers on paper."

Thirty days. One month. She picked up the unopened envelopes. They symbolized money lost. An urgency to start development on the app right away hit her, just as it had every day over the past six months. Her account balance showed little of her scrimping habits and as she thought about it, thirty days was much better than having to save for the next ten to twenty years.

"Okay. Call me when your people will be by."

Hanging up the phone, Meg laid her head on the desk, lifting and dropping it, repeating the action a few times. Who said doing something she loved wouldn't feel like work?

* * *

Keep reading Love, Austen.

9 781954 237155